i

BROKEN PROMISE

DEVIN DARNELL

DISCLAIMER

Acknowledgement

For the few people in my life who actually believes in me, I couldn't have accomplished this without you. Thank you.
G.D.H.

View other books by Devin Darnell at www.funkyfingersmedia.com

TABLE OF CONTENTS

Chapter 1 - PROMISE
The Dark Secret

"He doesn't care about me. All he cares about is getting some ass," I mumbled to myself, pulling the phone from my ear, staring at the dulled white ceiling in my bedroom. Brian had been bugging me all day at school about us moving to the next level in our relationship. I told him I wasn't ready so he decided to pelt me with a childish threat.

"If you don't do it, somebody else will," he replied, hanging up on me. Yet again, like most of the boys in school, he was only thinking about himself, putting his balls before his brain. He thought of me as the typical scarred sixteen-year-old virgin, but he was wrong.

Like everyone else, he didn't know the truth about my past, how I'd been carrying a dark secret since I was a little girl. Each time that I look into the mirror, I was reminded of what was done to me.

I remember the cool breeze that brushed against my face as I slept clutching my blanket, curled up in a knot. A noise coming from my cracked window woke me up in the middle of the night. I looked over to see what it was. The figure of a man climbing in! Paralyzed by fear, I closed my eyes tight and froze stiff, hoping he wouldn't see me. My arms started to shake as the sound of his footsteps shot like a gun through the dark air; creaking closer and closer to the bed. When he came to a stop, I could smell a liquored musk hovering above me. I peeled one of my eyes open to see him. To my surprise, it was a familiar face. He stood over me with a half-parted smile. I felt relief cool my whole body.

Excited to see him, I jolted up to give him a hug, but he quickly placed his hand on my shoulder.

"*Shhh*," he said, placing his finger over my mouth.

Without saying a word, he lifted my blanket and lay down next to me. The skin on my frail legs prickled as he touched them with his cold hands. A few moments later, I could hear the clacking sound of his belt buckle. I remember feeling confused. I knew something wasn't right, but I didn't know what and I didn't know what I could do. I wasn't afraid yet, just confused and uncomfortable.

He whispered in my ear, "Give me your hand." He shoved my hand down his pants. Surprised. Shocked. Warm. Wrong. I struggled to pull my arm back and found myself pinned and my mouth covered before I had even thought of screaming out for help. That night has haunted me my entire life.

Feeling the stress of the heated argument I had with Brian, I slithered off of the bed to retrieve a small tin box tucked away beneath my bed. The box was wrapped in a white towel stained with a few red spots. I slowly peeled the towel away, exposing the chipped and faded box cover.

Anticipation caused my leg to tingle, so I softly rubbed my hand up and down my inner thigh. After a few seconds, I hiked up my skirt, put the towel beneath my legs and opened the box. Carefully, I drew out a small knife hidden beneath my pictures and knickknacks. I set the blade on my inner thigh and slowly began to cut. The sting from the penetration shot from my leg up and down my whole body. Clenching my jaw, I closed my eyes and concentrated on the sensation. I sank into that sensation. The feeling gave me a high that numbed my pain. Just as I started to reach over to make a second cut, the phone rang. Its loud siren pierced the silent room and startling me. I dropped the knife on the floor. It fell—barely missing my foot. I grabbed the phone in haste desperately hoping that it was Brian.

2

"Hello," I answered, blotting my bleeding leg with the stained towel.

"Hey, baby, it's me," Brian answered; his mellow tone calmed my nerves.

"What do you want?" I replied.

"I wanted to say sorry."

I heard a scuffle on the line and a hollowed echo pitched into our ears.

"Promise!" It was Ma picking up the phone extension.

"Huh?" I asked.

"Get your ass down here and pick up these clothes you left on the floor. I told you about leaving your shit all over the house. And tell that little boy stop calling here after six."

"Alright, Ma. I'll be down in a minute."

She continued to curse before abruptly hanging up.

"I gotta go, Brian."

"Alright, I'll see you at school tomorrow," he said and hung up, gently this time.

I heard the front door open. The voice of my brother wafted through the air, shouting in pure excitement, "I got it Mom! I got it!"

"You got what, JJ?" Ma replied.

I put my box away and rushed down to the living room to see what all of the commotion was about.

"Read this," he said, handing her a letter. On the bottom corner of the envelope was a seal with the initials: HRU. The letter was titled, From the Office of Admissions, in bold print.

"Is this that letter you've been waiting for?" I asked.

"Yeah, baby sis," he said with a nervous tremble in his voice. JJ had been waiting for weeks to see if he'd receive a scholarship to play soccer for Harrison Reid University. It was one of the best Ivy League schools in the country. He knew he could write his own ticket if he could only get the chance to get in. We both anxiously waited as our mom read the letter through to the end. With a blank look on her face, she folded the letter and placed it back into the envelope.

"Well, did I get in?" JJ asked with bated breath.

"It said you made it," she grumbled.

Overjoyed, JJ let out a cheerful howl. He picked me up and twirled me around the room. He went over to Ma to hug her, but she placed her hand in his path, stopping him.

"Aren't you happy for me, Mom?"

"This don't mean a thing, JJ. All it's doing is delaying you from being out there on the corner with your brother. What you need is a full-time job since you're about to graduate. I done took care of your ungrateful ass for seventeen years; it's time for you to help pay some bills around here."

JJ's cheerful mood quickly faded away; his chest sunk in as if she'd just snatched his heart out. "Mom, Fred's been giving you and Daddy more than enough money to help out. If I go that'll be one less mouth to feed..."

Ma glared at him and gripped the letter in her hand, crinkling it. "If you go, don't come back, you hear? And don't even bother trying to get your daddy involved. This is my damn house, understand?"

"Understood," he said softly, looking down at the floor in disappointment.

"Look at me, boy," she said, flicking his head up by the chin. "I'm not playing with you. If you go, don't step foot back in this house," she pulled her hand back, jerking his head in the process.

At that moment the phone rang again. She whipped around turning her attention to me. "Don't even think about picking that phone up, Promise—I'll get it. If it's that boy, I'm gonna cuss his little fast ass out," she said and walked. She threw JJ's letter on the floor just before entering the kitchen.

JJ was speechless. The shock and disappointment set his face in stone. I approached him and patted him on the back.

"That's okay, J. I'm happy for you. You know she didn't mean what she said. She just mad because she wants you to stay, that's all."

"I know, baby sis. That's not what I'm upset about. I'm more worried about you and Kanna. While I'm gone, who's gonna look out for you two?"

My stomach dropped. I didn't realize it until the second he said it, but he was right. For the most part, JJ was the glue that held our family together. Our older brother Fredrick was never home. He spent most of his time out on the block selling drugs. His girlfriend, Patrice, lived with us on and off, but she stayed to herself when we were around. My dad had two jobs. He worked as a grocery store manager in the day and at night he was a security guard in an office building. Ma was supposed to be a housewife, but over the last few years she'd started spending more and more of her time away from us. We figured she was cheating on Dad. After he'd stumbled upon a used condom while cleaning out her car a year ago, he confronted her about it in private and never told us what she said. Since that day JJ had taken care of us. JJ would watch me and my little sister Kanna when Ma went out doing her dirt. J helped us with our homework and did everything else Ma and Dad were supposed to do for us as parents.

5

"We'll be okay, J. You need to get away from Janboro. All you've seen your whole life is this ghetto-ass neighborhood. Ohio will be a nice change from South Carolina," I said.

"I'm leaving next month on the 18th of June, Promise."

"Why so early?"

"The coach said if I got in he would set me up with a job so I can pay for some of the things I'm gonna need for the first semester. The job starts in June."

"I understand," I said, embracing him again. I wanted to persuade him to stay a little longer. I probably could have too, but deep down I knew that this was his only chance of getting out and doing something for himself. I had to make it as easy for him as I could.

"Promise, come ride with me. That was Sister Charles on the phone. She needs some help with her nephew's wedding arrangements," Ma shouted from the kitchen. Sister Charles was Ma's best friend from the church. Dad said the two of them where thick as thieves. She talked with Ma so much Dad believed that she had something to do with the affair. As I started on my way back to my room to change my clothes, I picked up JJ's letter from the floor.

"Go do it, big brother," I said, handing it to him.

He draped his arm around my neck and went upstairs with me. In a matter of moments, Ma was shouting for me.

"Girl, come on here," she yelled. JJ and I hurried down to meet her as she dragged out two large brown duffel bags and set them by the front door. "JJ, can you take these bags to the car for me, baby? Come on, Promise sweetheart," she said in a playful tone.

"Sister Charles must have given her a message from her man," I whispered to JJ. He agreed, nodding his head. The only time she talked that way was when she was getting what she

6

wanted. A call from her nigga on the side always made her bubbly.

Carrying one of the brown duffel bags on his back and the other on his side, JJ shuffled his way down our long rutted driveway to the car.

"JJ, tell your daddy me and Promise is going to spend the night over to Sister Charles's house. We'll be back in the morning. We'll talk more about that school thing later. Make sure Kanna is in the bed at nine and tell your brother to keep his ass out the house if he don't got his part of the rent. Love you, baby. Give Momma some suga," she said as JJ reluctantly hugged and kissed her cheek.

Chapter 2 -ALBERT
Last Straw

The day was only half over and I couldn't wait for it to end. Sitting in my small, smoke- filled office, I took one final glance at the application from the girl I was about to interview for the open position. As I looked over her work history, my desk intercom buzzed.

"Mr. Thomas?"

"Yes?"

"Your interview candidate is here."

"Can you send her to the break room and let her know I'll be right down?"

"Alright."

I tucked her application in my binder, straightened my tie and headed for the break room. The long walk down the narrow hallway gave me a chance to get my thoughts together but it didn't prepare me for what I was about to see when I opened the break room door. Inside, I was greeted by one of the most beautiful young ladies I'd ever seen. She was about five foot seven. She had a smooth, cocoa butter complexion with jet black hair that came down to her shoulders. A short blue business skirt and blazer sculpted and hugged a pear-shaped body. I guessed she had to be no more than 18 or 19. Her stature reminded me of my daughter, Promise.

"Hello, Mr. Thomas. I'm Stacey Lewis," she said, reaching out to shake my hand.

"Nice to meet you. Please have a seat," I replied quickly, trying to hide that I was glancing at her legs. She sat across the table from me; eyes wandering to the different posters and

8

plaques that lined the walls. "Sorry for the wait. I'm going to start with a couple of questions for you." I flipped open my binder and pulled out my check sheet. I was in the process of asking her the first question when there was a knock at the door.

"Mr. Thomas, sorry to interrupt you, but you have a call on line one. I think it's your brother. He says it's important."

"I'll take it in my office. Thanks, Mrs. Mattie." I nervously placed the check sheet back in the binder. "Sorry about this. Just sit tight. I'll be right back."

I hustled out of the room and up to my office. Butterflies churned in my stomach as I looked down at the hold button blinking on the phone. I suspected that the call could only be from what I feared would happen with my daughter Kanna spending the weekend over at his house. She wanted so badly to see her Uncle Andre and hang out with her cousin Nina. I had a feeling when he got her that it would reawaken his desire to end my marriage. We'd been arguing about the matter ever since JJ left for school. Gun shy, I finally picked up the phone prepared to hear an earful. "Mr. Thomas, speaking."

"Albert, it's me, Andre," I could hear the anger rumbling in his voice.

"What's wrong?"

"When I picked up Kanna today she was home alone."

"You must've just missed Diane, she probably ran to the corner store for something and left Kanna there so you could get her. What's the problem?"

He sarcastically chuckled. "Your wife is the problem. I guess that selfish bitch didn't notice the social service car parked in your neighbor's driveway?"

"I'm not gonna tell you again, don't talk about my wife that way. The social worker doesn't have anything to do with us. That's my neighbor's issue."

"It's a shame you're too blind to see it. What if the social worker saw Kanna open the door for me? They could've reported it, Albert. You could lose your daughters. Is that what it's going to take for you to quit Diane? Or, maybe you need her to cheat on you a few more times before you wise up."

"I told you, I'm not leaving her. How many times we gotta go through this? My house is fine; you need to worry about your own."

"If you still believe that, then you're a fool, baby brother. I've stood by and watched you take her shit for far too long. I'm not gonna let her get my nieces taken away from our family. If you won't do something about that whoring bitch, then I will."

"Fuck you."

I slammed the phone on the hook, shaking the desk in the process. My hands were jittering like I'd just come out of the frigid cold. I reached into my bottom drawer and pulled out a flask of gin. Sitting back in my chair, I took two swigs to help calm my nerves.

Andre always had a knack for upsetting me to the point of drinking; he was the self-righteous type, just like our father. Pop was pretty much the only person Andre looked up to. He respected him so much he treated Pop as if every word that came out of his mouth was the gospel. I knew if anyone was going to change his mind about the issue, it would be Pop. So I picked up the phone and called him. I told him what was going down. Pop assured me that he'd talk to Andre and straighten things out. After I hung up with him, a nervous giddy feeling snaked through my bones awaking my suspicions about Diane's disappearing act. She'd never left Kanna alone that way before; I had to go and find out why.

"Mrs. Mattie?" I buzzed.

"Yes sir?"

"I have a family emergency I have to deal with at home. Can you reschedule another interview for the young lady in the break room, and let her know I'm sorry for not returning."

"Sure thing, Mr. Thomas. I'll take care of it. I hope everything is alright," she said.

"Thanks, I hope so too." I took one final gulp from my flask, put it back in the drawer, and left.

I arrived home at around 2:00 p.m. Leaving my car, I slowly trudged up the driveway towards my ramshackle house. Walking onto the porch, I noticed a yellow paper tacked to the door. As I got closer, my eyes fixed on the bold words that read, *Eviction Notice.*

"Fuck!" I yelled, pounding my fist on the door. "I gave her the money. I can't believe she didn't pay the rent!" This was the third time over the last few months that Diane didn't pay. My heart began to pound so hard I could feel the vibration in my neck. Seeing the notice finally made me snap. The reality of my brother's premonition began to sink in. "She's not going to change," I said flinging the front door open and slamming it shut behind me.

"Diane," I shouted charging through the house in search of her. It was deathly quiet. All of the noise and commotion that usually filled the house that time of day was gone. In its place were only the echoed ticks of the grandfather clock in the living room. It was strange for a summer afternoon.

I wandered through the airy living room and into the kitchen. Once there I came upon a note on the table. It read: *Promise, be in the house by nine tonight. I'm over Sister Charles house. If your father calls, tell him I went to play bingo. Mommy.*

"We're about to get kicked out and she leave our child alone to go tricking? I can't do this anymore," I said, gritting my teeth in anger. There was only one thing on my mind I wanted to do and that was to confront her, but in order to do so, I would

11

have to go to a place I swore I'd never go again ... Sister Charles's house.

That house was Diane's hang out spot. It was the one place she knew I wouldn't come unannounced. I had discovered a used condom lying on the back seat in her car after one of her visits there. Ever since that happened, I assumed that Sister Charles's house was where she took her lover.

While rushing out the door to go back to my car, I came upon Promise walking up the stairs onto the porch. She was squinting in pain and rubbing her leg. "What's wrong, sweetie? What happened to you?"

"The little boy from up the street was riding his bike and ran right into me. I'm sore. I just need to put ice on it, that's all," she paused, giving me a twisted look. "Daddy, ain't you supposed to be at work?"

"Yeah, something's come up, sweetie."

"What's that sign on our door?"

I stood there speechless as she read it. Her face instantly filled with a look of total disgust. "I can't believe you guys didn't pay the rent again. Why we always gotta go through this?" she cried.

"Baby, I gave your mother the rent money. She just never paid it. She's at Sister Charles's house. I'm on my way over there to get this straight, okay? Don't worry. Everything is going to be alright. Now give me a hug." She was hesitant but eventually reached out and gave me a gentle squeeze. As we hugged, I whispered into her ear, "This will never happen again baby. Never, okay?"

"Okay," she replied softly.

"You go head in the house and put some ice on your leg before it gets worse." She looked up, wiped her eyes and went into the house. I watched as she slowly shut the door. It was really peculiar that Promise showed so much emotion toward this situation. It wasn't the first time we'd been evicted, so I assumed she was used to it. "I guess she's just as sick of this shit as I am," I mumbled, going to the car and starting it.

With my engine a go, I sat there for a moment and began to think about the *what if's*. Deep down, I knew there was a chance that some nigga would be there with Diane, and if that was the case, there wasn't a chance in hell that she or Sister Charles would open the door for me. I didn't want to drive halfway across town only to be turned away, so I came up with what I thought would be a perfect solution to my problem: Promise. *They'll open the door for her, and when they do, I'll be beside her waiting*, I thought.

In a flash, I turned the car off and raced back into the house to Promise's room. When I opened her door, I found her sitting on the floor, slouched over with her back towards me. I gave the door two quick knocks and entered the room. "Promise?" I called.

"What is it Daddy?" She nervously rustled around closing what sounded like a box. Being careful to keep it concealed she sprang to her feet and tossed it into her hamper.

"Promise, I need you to come ride with me to Sister Charles's house to get your mother."

She gave me a curious gaze.

"I'm waiting on a call from Brian, Daddy. We was supposed study tonight, remember? Mom had a bingo game tonight anyway. I don't think she's there."

"According to the note she left you, she is. You can still go meet him if we get back in time. This is more important. Come on here." As we headed for the door I started to have a feeling that I was forgetting something, and then remembered what it was. "Go on out to the car, Promise. I'm going to leave a note for your brother and Patrice and then I'll be right out."

13

Once she was gone, I went upstairs to our bedroom and got my gun. It was a Berretta 8000 with a hair pin trigger, guaranteed to scare a motherfucker if they tried to break bad. I tucked it in my belt, covered it with my shirt and left.

Sister Charles lived on the other side of town in Vista. It was like Beverley Hills when compared to where we lived in Swansboro. Every house in her neighborhood was expensive. Most of the people who lived there were upper class snobs who took care of their own. Any other day in Vista would've probably been your typical all-American Mayberry day, but today it was about to get real hood.

We arrived around dusk. I slowed the car trying to get a good view of the house from a distance but was blinded by the flickering sunlight through the trees.

"I told you, Ma might not even be there. It's Friday, so they usually be at bingo around this time, Daddy," Promise pleaded, attempting to get me to turn back.

"Listen. I'm going to drop you off in front of the house. I want you to knock on the door. If somebody answers before I park, just tell them a friend dropped you off."

"Why don't you just park and we can go up there together?"

"I can't, sweetheart. I'm sorry. This is the only way I'll get a chance to talk to your mom and it's important that I do because I don't want to lose you or your sister."

"What are you talking about, Daddy? How are you going to lose us?"

"I'll explain later. Just do this for me, baby?"

"Alright," she answered in an uneasy tone.

14

"Now, listen. You go in first. When I knock on the door, I want you to open the door for me if no one else does. Okay, sweetie?"

"Okay," I could see the fear in her eyes. She began to rock back and forth, something she's done since she was a little girl whenever she was afraid or nervous.

I reached out and held her hand. "Don't worry, Promise. I'm not going to hurt your mother. You have my word."

"I know," she whimpered as if she were a much younger girl.

I dropped her off in front of the house and quickly pulled off, hoping no one would see me. I parked behind Diane's car which was one door down the street. I could see Promise slowly making her way up the driveway to Sister Charles's front door. She stood at the doorstep for a second before she worked up the nerve to knock. Within moments someone opened the door but I couldn't see who it was. Promise stood there for a few seconds then finally went into the house.

When the front door shut, I got out of my car and crept my way up the driveway, ducking under the windows of the house right up to the front door. I knocked on the door, being careful to stand away from the peephole. I could hear Diane's big mouth from inside the house.

"Stop, Michael," she said in a playful voice. Hearing that, I began to feel sick to my stomach. My head began to throb.

I have to stay calm for my daughter, I coached myself.

"Who is it?" a man answered in a deep baritone voice.

"It's your neighbor from 1711," I replied trying to lower my voice so Diane wouldn't recognize me.

When the door opened, a tall muscular young guy who looked no older than 24 stood there. He had his shirt off; it was draped over his shoulders. Both of his arms were covered with

15

tattoos of red flames that twisted all the way up to the back of his neck. *So this is who she's fucking,* I thought while sizing him up.

"How can I help you, brotha?" he asked.

"Hurry up, Michael. I need you," Diane playfully chided from a distant room.

"Aight, give me a second!" he answered with a goofy grin.

My heart began to race. The sound around me was drowning into white noise. I could see him mouthing words but couldn't make out what he was saying. I stood there like a statue of stone, only focused on the shitty smirk that was on his baby face. A few moments had passed and I'd still not answered him.

"Yo, can I help you with som-en?" he said, motioning to shut the door.

All of a sudden I lost it. I pulled the gun out of my belt, grabbed it by the barrel and swung at him. He darted back, causing me to miss. Stumbling and off balance, I dropped to one knee. Seeing his chance to strike, he lunged at me. As he began to descend I swung again, this time hitting him on the throat. He fell to the ground clenching his neck, gasping for air.

Filled with rage I stood there, gun in hand and now pointing it at him, peering down at the man as he tried to catch his breath.

"What was that?" someone yelled from inside the house. I began to hear a commotion followed by the clacking of footsteps coming to the door. I could see the reflection of figures on the hardwood floors that lined the white-pillared entryway of the house. The shadows seem to move into the main room in slow motion. Once they made it into the entryway, the first face I saw was Promise, followed by Diane, Sister Charles and two other women I hadn't seen before. One of the women looked to be in her mid to late fifties, while the other looked to be in her twenties. The younger of the two women ran to the guy lying on the ground.

"What did you do?" she cried. "He shot him? I'm here, baby, I'm here. Somebody call an ambulance!" she screamed.

"What did you do, Albert?" Diane screamed. "What did you do?"

"Are you fucking him?" I snarled.

"Fucking him? You shot him because you thought that I was fucking him? This is Sister Charles's nephew. He was going with us to bingo tonight. That's his fiancée," she said, pointing to the pale-faced young lady in a state of a shock kneeling by her man.

"I'm going to call an ambulance," Sister Charles said.

"I'm okay. He didn't shoot me. I'm alright," the young man replied.

Promise shook her head in disbelief at what she just witnessed. Seeing that, I quickly put the gun back in my belt and reached out for her hand. She smacked my hand away and stomped back into the room they had all come out from.

"I'm calling the police on you. That was assault," the fiancée said, helping her lover to his feet.

"We need to go somewhere and talk," I said, grabbing Diane by the arm. I pulled her out the door and down to the sidewalk.

"Albert, I'm not going anywhere with you," she said, yanking her arm back. "I know you're here because of your punk ass brother. I bet he got your head all gassed up telling you that I'm still cheating on you, and your dumb ass believed it. I told you I'm not seeing that guy anymore. It's over between me and him. He's not man enough to take care of his—" she paused, covering her mouth with her hands.

"He's not man enough to take care of his what? Go head, finish what you were about to say," I replied, pulling her hands down.

17

"I'm through talking," she rolled her eyes and started back toward the house. I ran after her, stopping her as she opened the door.

"I'm not leaving until you tell me what the hell you were about to say."

"I was going to say he's not man enough to take care of his responsibilities."

"What's that mean?"

"It means I'm pregnant and I'm not sure if it's yours!"

Chapter 3 - ANDRE
High School Sweethearts

If ever there was an evening that I needed some peace and quiet, it was this one. Whenever I was stressed I normally took solace in the comfort of my living room, but it wasn't available. It had been taken over by my daughter and niece who were having a slumber party, so I went to the next best place: my back porch. I sat alone on my old wooden rocker listening to the echoes of the cicadas chirping in the oncoming night. I rocked back and forth, attempting to let the cool summer breeze put my mind at ease, but it wasn't working. The frustration with my brother was just too damn hard to shake.

Sensing that my time on the porch was only making matters worse, I got up and went inside to put the girls down for bed. Both girls huddled under a pair of plush sofa pillows with their eyes glued at a program on TV.

"After this show goes off, y'all go to bed. It's getting late," I said to them.

"No it's not, Uncle Andre. It ain't even all the way dark outside," Kanna replied.

"Yeah, Dad, we don't have school tomorrow. Can we watch one more movie? Please?"

"I said no, Nina. After this show goes off, y'all clean this living room up and go to bed."

"Yes, Dad."

"Goodnight, sweet pea," I went over and kissed her forehead.

"What about me?" Kanna said.

"You know I'll never forget about you, sunshine," I walked over and kissed her forehead as well.

"I love coming over here. I wish I could come over here all the time."

"I wish you could too, sunshine. I wish you could too. Goodnight and don't let the bed bugs bite," I said, tickling her sides and making her laugh. Seeing Kanna as happy as she was was food for my soul. With every smile and giggle, I knew that it took her mind further away from what awaited her at home after the weekend was over.

I went up to my bedroom and eased onto the bed. The thoughts in my head spun around like a pinwheel. A few moments later the door opened and my wife walked in. She'd just gotten out of the shower. She was humming a tune with her head cocked to the side, blotting her hair dry. Seeing my face, she stopped. "What's wrong?" she asked.

"I'm so sick of this shit, Nicky. He just won't see the light of day."

"What are you talking about, babe?"

"Albert. I can't get him to budge from that woman. It's like she's put a root on him or something."

"Well, he's a grown man. Let him be with her. He'll learn the hard way. Sometimes that's the only way people learn," she said.

"I wish it was that simple, babe. If it was just them two, I probably could accept that, but those kids are in the middle and I feel responsible for that. If it wasn't for me, Albert wouldn't even be with Diane. I was selfish. That's the only reason I hooked them up."

"How's that?"

20

I told her the story… We were teenagers in school when it happened. The school's homecoming game was one of the biggest events each year. After the game, most of the upperclassmen would throw a big party that everyone wanted to go to. That particular year I was voted homecoming king, so the most important thing on my mind was making sure I looked good. One afternoon, I went to the mall and saw this nice, expensive suit. It was a glossy pearl color with cufflinks to match. Looking at the way it shone in the sunlight, I had to have it, so I picked up a job at Saul's deli off of Jaboro Street to get part of the money I needed for the suit. Pop gave me the other half of the money, but with one condition. I had to take Albert with me to the game.

Albert was extremely shy and introverted. Pop thought he was a little off for staying in the house as much as he did, so he wanted me to help start getting him out more. In his eyes it was the best of both worlds. He figured if Albert went out with me, then that would help keep me out of trouble. When the night of the game came I began to worry about how Albert was going to ruin all my plans. The last thing I needed was my introverted brother scaring all the girls away. So I paced my room, trying to come up with a solution. I pleaded with Pop to let me go alone, but all my words fell on deaf ears. Time ticked away and before I knew it, it was 5:00 p.m., two hours before the game, and I still hadn't come up with anything. I paced and paced until finally it hit me. I'd find Albert a date, someone who would help keep him off my back and away from me. I got on the phone and called up my boy's girl, Evette. She was known for having a lot of girlfriends. "Hey, Evette. This is Andre. I need a big favor."

"What is it?" she scoffed.

"I need you to ask one of your girlfriends to go with my brother to the game and the party tonight. I need someone who can keep him occupied, if you know what I mean."

"Keep him occupied? I ain't no pimp."

"Not occupied like that. Just someone who can keep him from being up under me all night."

"Why you calling me now? You should've told me about this earlier. It's the night of the game, Dre. You know everybody has someone they're going with."

"I know it's short notice, but if you can find someone for him, I'll owe you."

"Okay, I'll see if my little cousin can go. She's a little goofy, but other than that she's alright. The only thing is her momma might not let her go. The two of them have been going at it lately."

"Just try for me."

"I will, just make sure he looks halfway decent. Don't have my cousin with someone dressed like a corn ball."

"Don't worry, he'll be sharp. I'll see you there." I went up the stairs to our room, straight to the closet to rummage through our hand-me-down clothes. It took a while but eventually I found him something decent to wear.

We left the house around 6:30 that evening. We were running so late that I barely made it on time to get into position for the homecoming parade. Once there, I placed my crown on my head and hopped aboard my float. As I rode across the football field, I could see Evette with a tall, skinny girl next to her, sitting at the very top of the bleachers next to my brother. After the parade was over I went up to join them in the stands to watch the rest of the game. For the better part of the time, Albert kept to himself. Occasionally, I'd catch him snapping his head around to get a few looks at the girls but that was as far as it got. When the game was over, Albert and I caught a ride with one of my friends to the after party. The party was at a huge lodge that a couple of the upperclassmen pooled money for and rented.

Walking in the front doors of the lodge, we were met by Evette and the tall girl from the game. "This is my cousin,

Diane." Albert stood next to me as if Diane was going to jump out and bite him on the ass.

"Diane, you have to excuse my brother's behavior. He hasn't really been out with a girl before."

She giggled softly below her breath. Embarrassed, Albert gave me a swift shove. "Forget you, Andre. I've been out plenty of times," he said.

"Well, show me then. Show me you not scared. I dare you to dance with her," I nudged him over to her.

Panic filled his face. He was so tense I could see the sweat starting to bead on his forehead. *What have I done?* I thought, feeling that I'd pushed him too far. I just knew things were about to go downhill from there, so I went to yank him aside to save what little dignity he had left, and that's when he surprised me.

Albert grabbed Diane by the hand, whispered into her ear and then pulled her out onto the dance floor. I was shocked. The rest of the night went by real smooth. A few of the guys got ahold of a master key to the lodge, so we had three back rooms in case one of the fellas needed a little more privacy to do what most teenage boys wanted to do. In the process of leaving, Evette and I found Albert and Diane in one of those rooms hooking up. After that night, Albert became a dreamy eyed, pussy-whipped fool for that girl.

As the weeks passed, they got more serious about each other, so Albert brought her home and introduce her to Pop. For some reason, Pop took a liking to Diane from the first time he saw her. When it came to Diane, he let that bitch do things that I never believed that he would, things like spending the night. She'd stay and she or Albert didn't hear a peep out of Pop. That's how she got pregnant with Fred in the 12th grade.

"Now look at Albert," I told Nicky. "After all these years and four kids later, Diane doesn't respect him. She's probably fucking every guy with two dollars in Jansboro. He has a drug dealer son and can barely afford to keep food on the table for the two kids he has left to raise. If I'd gone to that party with him and just hung out rather than pushed him off on her, none of this shit would've happened."

"This isn't your fault, baby. You and your brother are two different people. You both came from the same house. He just chose to take a different road than you."

"It's still no excuse for the kids to suffer. I sat by and watched Fred go down the wrong path, assuming he would turn out more like JJ. Now Promise is damn near certain to follow in the same direction as Fred if someone doesn't step in and do something, babe. I can't let those kids grow up like that anymore. There was a social service car parked in the neighbor's driveway today when I went to pick up Kanna. She was at the house all alone when I got there. Diane left her without a care. I told Albert about it and he gave me the same bullshit answer. He's lucky Kanna is all right. The poor child could've burned the house down."

"Dre, I know what you wanna do. You know I don't have a problem with Kanna staying with us."

"You already know how I feel about Promise," I said.

"I know," she nodded.

"I'll talk to Albert about it when I drop Kanna off on Monday. He can't see it, but Diane is going to drive that house into the ground."

"Daddy, Big Daddy is here!" Nina yelled from downstairs.

"Why is Pop over here this time of night?"

"I don't know, but I'm going to bed, sweetie. Tell him I said hi," Nicky yawned rolling the sheets back.

As I walked down the darkened stairway, I saw the small figure of someone sitting on the bottom step. It was Nina. She was crouched over, grasping her legs with her arms. Her head rested on her knees. I touched her back to get her attention.

"What's wrong, Nina?"

She jumped as if I'd pricked her with a needle. "Nothing. Daddy I'm just tired," she said.

"You sure?"

"I'm sure."

"Where's Kanna?"

"She's in the kitchen with Grand Daddy."

"Alright. Well, go on up and get in the bed."

"Okay, Daddy," she scurried up the stairs with her arms folded one over the other.

In the kitchen, there was Pop with Kanna on his knee playing motorcycle as he always did with the kids. Kanna laughed while Pop repeatedly bounced her in the air off his knee.

"You're too old to be doing that, sweetie. Get off Grand Daddy's leg," I said.

"Junior, I don't mind. She ain't never too old to ride on Big Daddy's knee," he smiled.

"I know Pop, but it's her bedtime. Kanna, go on up. Nina will show you where the extra blankets are."

Pop lifted her off his knee. "You tell Nina I'm upset she ain't come give me some sugar. Big Daddy needs that to live on," he told Kanna.

"Okay, I will. Goodnight, Big Daddy. Goodnight, Uncle Andre."

"Goodnight," he replied, tapping her backside.

When Kanna left I could feel the tension in the room rise. His matter-of-fact demeanor intensified when he pulled out his pipe and began to load it with tobacco. "I need to talk to you, Junior. Have a seat," he said in his raspy voice.

I sat in the chair next to him. "What's up, Pop?"

"Diane and Albert told me about what you said to them. Junior, what goes on in their house is their business. If they need help from me, you or anybody, then let them ask. Leave them alone and tend to your own house. I taught you better than this."

"Pop, you don't know what's going on."

"Andre," he said in a raised voice, getting to his feet. "If you talk to them again I suggest you apologize to your brother and Diane. I hear that you're talking bad about her. That's your brother's old lady; it's about time you start treating her like your family."

"Pop, Albert didn't tell you that he found out that Diane was cheating. That woman been playing him for a fool."

He looked down at the floor, put his pipe in his mouth and began to chew on the bud of it. "Junior, like I said, it's none of our business. Let them figure it out."

I rose to my feet. "What do you mean, none of our business? He's your son and my brother. He needs us because he's afraid of that scandalous ass bitch."

"Sit your ass down, Junior," he said, gritting his teeth.

With my knees quivering, I simply stood there looking into his bloodshot eyes.

"Did you hear me, boy? I said, sit your ass down, Junior," he repeated.

I slowly sat back down. He cracked a match, lit his pipe and took a few puffs. "Like I said, you gone leave them be and

26

stay out of they business, and the first chance you get I want you to call Diane and apologize to her. Are we clear?"

"Yes, sir. We're clear."

Chapter 4 - FREDRICK
Everyday Grind

I was having one of my best nights slanging on the block. The weed heads were coming out every hour on the hour all day long. To make it even better, I hadn't even seen a single pig ride by. I was going to call it a night until I saw one of my best customers drive up. His name was Matthew but I called him Prep School. A white boy from uptown, he drove a souped-up neon orange Subaru sports car with an ugly-ass spoiler on the back. He was goofy as hell but I didn't give a fuck. As long as his money was green, that was all that mattered to me. I got up off the stoop and approached his car.

"Waddup, Prep?"

"Hey, Freddy. What do you have tonight, dude?"

"All I have is two more left. I got some Hydro. That'll run you fifteen, or you can get some of that Reggie Miller for ten."

"I don't know, man. I hear that regular stuff you have is strong. I gotta think about it." "It's hot out here tonight. Come on, dog. Make up your mind."

"Give me the Hydro."

"Aight. Wait here."

He waited patiently while I ran across the street to the back alley to get my last two bags of weed. I stashed them in an old tin can hidden between two garages. As I made my way back to the car, it began to drizzle. We did our exchange disguised as a handshake.

"Aight. Good looking out, Prep. An' yo, let your friends know I'll have some more yayo soon. I have little, but my boy should have my re-up any day now."

"I'll let them know. Your powder is way better than that shit that Yasif is selling in Dreighton."

"Yeah, his shit is garbage. That fake gangsta don't know good product. Keep coming to me and I'll keep you straight."

"You always do, Freddy. I have to go, man. My lady has been calling me all day. I need to go take care of that if you know what I mean," he chuckled.

"Aight, dog. Go take care of your business. I'll holla at you Tuesday."

He pulled off, engine roaring and music blazing. Watching his taillights fade into the night, I found myself wishing that I had his life. *How could he waste his fucking trust fund on weed every other day? If only...*

I'd sold most of what I had, so it was time for me to punch the clock and head home to my baby. I took the same precautions every day before I shut down shop. I went back to the alley and placed the last bag of Reggie Miller along with the cash in my wallet and tucked it in my boxers by my dick, a place where Jansboro PoPo usually wouldn't pat down too heavy handed. The drizzle that was coming down quickly turned into rain and I hurried back to my car as the rain started to pour.

Second to Patrice, my car was the love of my life. The 1979 baby blue Mustang was my only escape from the everyday grind. I looked forward to the nightly drive home I had in her. It gave me a chance to think about my big plans of moving to Hollywood. My nights of hustling were finally starting to pay off. All I needed was another two G's and I'd be out of the three-story spinach-green hellhole that I called home.

Arriving home, I saw Ma sitting on the front porch crying. She had on that tan-colored body suit that she usually

29

wore when she was going out to the club. *What could be wrong? This ain't like her,* I thought, slowly approaching the porch. She was sitting on my father's old wooden work stool with a half-drunk bottle of Jack Daniels in hand.

"You okay, Ma?"

She continued to cry, so I reached out for her. She pushed me away and began to talk in a somber, low tone, slurring her words.

"No, I'm not okay. Your dad and I had a fight today at Sister Charles's house. We're splitting up."

"Y'all been through this already. Ma? He forgave you for all that bullshit you did. Why can't you let this other guy go?"

"It ain't that simple, Fredrick. Things a little more complicated now," she bucked back the bottle of Jack, draining it dry. Standing to her feet, she tossed the empty bottle into the front yard then slowly wobbled her way across the porch toward the door. I noticed her hands were trembling.

"How is it complicated, Ma? What mo' aren't ya saying?"

"Drop it, Fredrick. We have worse things to worry about right now."

"Ma, what is it? Did Pop do something to you? Did he hit you?"

"Fredrick LaTray Thomas, I swear, boy, if you don't leave this alone I'm going slap your little ass back into the middle of next week. You need to worry about where we're going to live because your damn daddy didn't pay the rent. Look at the door," she pointed to the yellow form that was tacked on the front door.

In that moment I could feel my dream of moving starting to slip away. All of my hustling and planning was going to shit. The last time we got evicted I had to put up all my money to help get us a place to live. That nightmare was starting to happen all over again.

"Ma, I gave you money each month to put toward bills. What happened to the money I gave you? You gave it to that nigga, didn't you? Is that something else he took from you when he played you for pussy? Our rent money?"

She quickly came towards me, reached back and slapped me. The force of it was so hard I could feel the back draft from the wind her hand carried. "Don't you ever, in your life, talk to me that way. First and foremost, I am your mother. I brought you into this world. Disrespect me again like that and I'll take you out of it. You think since you're out here selling your little weed and driving a nice car that makes you a fucking man? You don't become a man until you live out on your own and get a real job. You still under my roof. Don't forget that."

I looked up at her, ears ringing and face stinging. Inside I was furious, but I kept my composure. I knew most of her behavior was from the alcohol so it wasn't worth getting into it with her right now, but she would have to answer for all that missing money later.

"Ma, I apologize for being disrespectful. I ain't mean to raise my voice. I just wanted to know what happened to the money I gave you to put toward the rent. That's all."

"You ought not to be questioning me. Your jailbird father supposed to be the man of the house. Go downtown and ask him. "

"What are you talking about, Ma? Are you saying Dad's locked up?"

"I don't want to talk about this no more."

"Ma, what's going on?" I asked. She cut her eyes back at me, clenching her fist. "Never mind," I said, still feeling the sting from her last slap. I needed to just let it go until she sobered up.

"Ma, why don't you come in the house with me? It's hot out here; the mosquitoes must be eating you alive."

"No, you go ahead. I'm going out with Mannie tonight." Just as she said that he pulled up. Mannie was her flamboyantly gay roll bitch that she went out with on occasion.

"Come on, girl," he yelled from the car. She trotted down, got in and they pulled off.

Gotta find out what's going on with Dad. I went into the house and called the city jail. After a few moments of checking, the clerk found him in the system. He was being held on an assault charge. His bail was five thousand dollars. That was nearly half of what I had saved.

"You'll have to be here in the next half hour. If not, he's going to have to stay over the weekend until Monday morning," the clerk said.

Dad had to work the weekend. He'd lose his job if he didn't show, and that was the last thing we needed.

"No, I'll be there in time, thanks."

The city jail was on the other side of town. If I was going to make it, I had to hurry. I ran up to the bathroom to get some cash I had hidden in a secret spot in the wall. In the process of leaving I found a note on the counter left by my girlfriend. I placed it in my pocket along with the cash and left. Speeding off from the house, my mind was moving a mile a minute. Pressed for time, I knew the only way I was going to make it to the jail on time was by going through the projects of Dreighton Heights. It was my old stomping ground before this Haitian drug man named Yasif claimed the territory. He didn't like it when outsiders came through unannounced, especially an outsider who slanged. Driving into this hood was going to be risky, but I didn't have much of a choice.

As I approached the abandoned project streets, I turned my radio down, attempting to avoid attention while I passed through. I was almost out when I came to a stop light. While waiting for the light to change I pulled out my money and started to separate what I needed for the bail. Shuffling through my crumpled cash, Tricy's note dropped out onto my lap. I picked the note up, placed it on the seat next to me and continued to count the money. I was just about done when the light turned green. Having my money still in hand, I paused. The two cars behind me began to beep their horns so I pulled over to the side of the road to finish up. I counted the last few bills, separated the cash and put it back into my pocket. I picked up the note from the seat and started to place it in my pocket as well. *Better see what she wants*, I thought opening the folded paper.

It read, "Me and Promise went out to get something to eat. Be right back." It was signed, *Love Patrice*. It wasn't anything special. She just wanted to let me know where she was going. I smiled, thinking about how sweet my girl was, how throughout all my bullshit she stuck by me. Since I met Patrice, she'd cleaned herself up and kicked her coke habit—that alone proved to me how much she loved me. This is why I wanted to leave town and start something new with her. Sitting on the side of the road I thought about what my mom said about a real man living on his own, she was right. It'd finally become clear to me that I had a choice, and for once, I was going to choose myself.

"Fuck it. I love you, Dad, but this ain't my problem. I'm using my money to leave this shit hole tomorrow," I said out loud. Overjoyed at my decision, I couldn't wait to get home to tell Patrice. I kissed the note, placed it back into my pocket, and swung the car around to go home. I got as far as a block before noticing that there was a black van following me. Looking in my rearview, I tried to see who and how many there were in the van, but I could only see the figures of the driver and passenger.

At every corner I turned, they got closer and closer. Trying to lose them, I quickly turned down a back alley. The van screeched on its brakes, stopping in the middle of the street, blocking the alley way. I put my foot on the gas and kept going. Roaring through the alley I hit a deep pothole and lost control of the car. I swerved over and smashed into a row of trash cans that lined the back of the fence. I could hear the sounds of glass and metal clanking followed by a loud hiss from the engine. The car rolled for a second before coming to a stop under a street light.

"Shit!" I yelled, trying to catch my breath. I turned the key, attempting to see if the car would start. The engine sputtered then cranked up. I looked back in the rearview to see if the van was still there, but it had gone.

"Let me get the fuck outta here," I said. I drove up and turned onto the street at the opposite end of the alley. Coming to the street's intersection I began to hear the hissing noise again. I looked down at my gauges; the car was overheating. All of a sudden a ball of smoke rose from the hood. The engine shook violently and shut off. Just as I went to turn the key to see if it would start, I saw the glow of headlights rolling up from behind me. It was the van. I pumped the gas pedal over and over, turning the key.

"Start, dammit, start!" I screamed. Three men jumped out of the van, all of them reaching for handguns. Two of the men rushed to my door while the other stood at the passenger side with his gun fixed on me.

"Get out the car, nigga," one of the men yelled, pulling at my locked door.

The man on the passenger side yanked at his door. "He ain't open it. Smoke his ass, Tooch!" he shouted back at the two at my door. The man closest to me cocked his gun.

"Wait, wait, you can have it man, take it!" I yelled. I unlocked the door and got out. The larger of the two men slammed me to the ground and placed his gun at the temple of my head. The other man jumped in the car and unlocked the passenger door for the third man.

"It won't start, my nigga," the wheel man said.

34

"Yo, leave that shit be, get his set." In a flash they ripped the tape deck out.

"I got it, get the business from him!"

"Aight, she said it's in his wallet," said the man with the gun to my head. He yanked me up. "Strip, motherfucker. Take everything off!"

"I don't got nothing on me, man."

He punched me in the face. "Take your clothes off, nigga before I smoke your ass."

I quickly shed my shirt, pants and shoes.

"I said everything. I know where you hide it," the gun man said, pointing to my boxers.   "Come on, dog. Don't shoot me like this."

He pressed the gun against my temple even harder. "Take 'em off."

I pulled down my boxers. My wallet fell to the ground. "I got it, let's go my nigga," he said.

"Yo, jackpot," one of the other men said, pulling the cash from my pants pocket. He turned to the other. "Earn your stripes, my nigga. Off that motherfucka."

In that second I lunged for his gun, but missed. The next thing I saw was a muzzle flash and I dropped to the ground.

"D.H. bitch, stay the fuck from round here," one said, running back to the van. They drove off, leaving me there—laid out in the street.

Chapter 5 - PATRICE
Trip to the Moon

My rendezvous with Tasha was becoming a guilty pleasure. Like so many days before, I found myself lying on her oversized bed pining for more of the good sex that she had been giving me.

"Bring that ass here," she said, wrapping her arms around my quivering legs, splitting them apart. I closed my eyes and could feel her soft wet lips slowly kissing up my thighs.

"Right there," I said, letting out a moan when she reached the spot. Her tongue slithered back and forth, driving me insane.

"You like that?" she teased.

"Oh, shit… I like that," I lustfully cried in the midst of my climax. A tingling sensation pulsated through me, followed by a paralyzing rush. I gasped, clutching the satin pillow next to me, relishing the high until my body calmed.

"You could have this every day if you wanted to," she said, snuggling beside me.

"Damn, that'd be nice, but you know it wouldn't work. All we got in common is fucking. I belong to Fred now. To be honest, I think I'm starting to love him."

At that very second, her demeanor changed to cheerless. She scooted away, leaving me tittering on the edge of the bed. "Patrice, you know falling in love with him won't be good for either one of you. What the hell do you see in that boy anyhow?"

"I don't know, Tasha. I guess I'm a sucker for thugs. I also feel like I can tell him anything."

"So why can't you tell him about us? If he loves you, he'll understand."

"Don't be mad. You know my situation ain't easy. What I'm doing for my cousin is making it hard enough. Bringing you into it would only make things worse."

"I aint mad. I just want you to be careful. I don't like that double agent shit your cousin got you doing."

"Don't worry, I'll have what I need soon. I know where Fred keeps it now, I just have to figure out a way to get it."

"Don't let Fred find out what you're doing."

"He won't, Tasha." I eased back closer and gave her a peck on the cheek. "It's time for me to go. I gotta get back before Fred gets home." I leaned forward, poking the crumpled covers in search of my clothes between the sheets. Out of the corner of my eye, I could see Tasha reaching behind the lamp on the night stand. She retrieved a small glass mirror with a powder-filled plastic baggy resting on top. I quickly turned away when I realized what she was about to do. I scrambled, picking my clothes from the sheets piece by piece while being tortured by the tapping sound that she was making behind me. It became unbearable to stand so I turned and huffed in an attempt to get her to stop. She gazed back at me with a devilish grin.

"You have to do that right now?" I asked.

"Do a line with me before you go," was her answer, holding the mirror with three separated lines of coke.

"I can't. I told Fred I was going to stop."

"He ain't here. Come on… just do one." She handed me one end of a straw she'd cut in half. It had only been a month since I last touched the stuff. It was my weakness and she knew as long as she was the only person offering it that I wasn't going anywhere. I stood there, trying my best to fight the mouth-watering hunger I had inside.

37

"Uh oh, I guess he got a leash on you," she said, grabbing the straw from my hand.

"Fuck it. I'll do one," I replied, yanking it back. I leaned down, pressed one nostril and snorted the first line. That familiar sense of euphoria hit me instantly.

"That's my nigga," Tasha laughed. "Go head and finish it off," she said, pushing me on.

"I can't. I really can't. I gotta go," I said in a daze trying to force my brain back into being sober.

Smacking her lips, she took the mirror and the straw from me. "Give me a call later if you can, alright?"

"Alright."

I left her house feeling like I was floating on air. My lack of balance made it nearly impossible to walk on the cracked and uneven sidewalk that wended through the neighborhood. After staggering a few times, I stepped down into the street along the flat concrete gutter and carried on my way. Fred's place was a half-mile walk from Tasha's. I made it only few blocks when a car approached me. I could tell that it was Fred's granddad from the car's mustard yellow exterior and half hung bumper.

"Hey, where you headed? I'll give you a ride," he asked, rolling in beside me.

"I'm going to the house. I'm aight."

"Oh, good. I'm going that way too. Come on, you'll sweat to death in this heat." He had an uneasy demeanor about him, which made me nervous, but faced with the long dizzying walk ahead I took him up on the offer and got in.

"So, how's my grandson treating you?"

"He treat me good."

"Well, that's what I like to hear," he pulled a cigarette from his top pocket and placed it in his mouth. "My damn cigarette lighter is broke. You mind reaching in the glove compartment and getting me a match?" While I reached down to open the glove box, he flicked the radio on and changed it to an oldies station.

"Here you go," I said, handing him the box of matches.

"I'm driving. Can you light it for me?" I struck the match and put it up to the cigarette. He inhaled, igniting its red glow. "Thanks, sweetheart," he replied, blowing the flame out.

"You're welcome," I scoffed, throwing the match out the window.

"I see you and my grandson still staying at the house with the rest of the family?"

"Yeah, for now."

"I hope you ain't too panicked about the eviction. Those kind of things gotta way of working itself out."

"Eviction? What eviction?"

He cut his eye over at me. "Damn, baby girl. You must not have gone home today. Sheriff dropped it off earlier. Y'all gotta be out in five days."

"I told Fred that this would happen. His mom is always fucking shit up."

"Hold on there, sweetheart. Don't go throwing the blame, expecting a blind person to catch it. You don't know what happen," he quipped.

"*Hmm*, okay."

A cold silence fell between us. He went on smoking his cigarette and crooning a song that played on the radio. I could tell that I hit a nerve and I welcomed the dissatisfaction that it gave him. When we finally reached the house I was anxious to go inside.

"Thanks for the ride," I said, unlatching the door to get out. He placed his hand on my knee to stop me.

"If you staying under Diane's roof, you best to show some respect. Ain't nothing in this world free, not even for a cute little thing like you," he gently squeezed my knee.

"Goodnight, Mr. Andre." I pushed his hand from my knee, got out the car and rushed into the house.

"Asshole," I mumbled, shutting the door behind me.

My high was starting to wear off. I could feel my nerves getting jittery for more. The sample size that I got from Tasha had awakened an unwavering thirst that needed to be quenched.

I just need a little taste, that's all, I thought feverishly walking upstairs, headed for the bathroom.

The last stash of coke Fred hid in the house was in the bathroom in a hole in the wall behind the medicine cabinet. As I came upon the cracked bathroom door, I could hear someone sensually groaning. Curious to see who it was, I peeked through the crack of the door and saw Promise sitting on the side of the tub. She was holding a small brown handled kitchen knife; its blade was stained with blood. She pulled the knife down and methodically cut into the flesh on her thigh.

"What the hell are you doing?" I shouted, bursting in. Startled, she dropped the knife in the tub.

"*Ah...* I was... How did you ... I mean why did you come in here? I was using the bathroom in private," she stuttered.

"No, it looks like you were slicing your leg in private."

"Just go, get out," she cried, pushing me towards the door.

40

"No, Promise, I ain't going nowhere till you give me that knife."

She stubbornly crossed her arms and turned away from me, ignoring that I was there. After a few moments had passed, blood began to drip down her leg. She snatched a towel from under the sink and lifted her dress to wipe the wound. I looked on in horror as she blotted the blood from two gruesomely scarred thighs.

"How long have you been doing this, Promise?" I asked, kneeling down beside her. She looked down at me. "You can tell me. I won't tell nobody." She began to form words but hesitated talking. "Trust me, this is between me and you. How long?"

She exhaled shaking her head to and fro. "I been doing it for a while now, off and on."

"Why?"

"I don't know. Because it feels good."

"Cutting yourself feels good?"

"You don't understand. It's like when I do it, I feel numb. It makes me forget about days like this."

"Days like this? What happened?"

She opened her mouth to answer but her words where choked away with emotion. Overwhelmed, she buried her head on my shoulder and started to cry.

"It's alright, tell me what happen," I said, gently rubbing her back in an attempt to comfort her.

"It's my daddy. He got into a fight over Sister Charles's house and now he's locked up. He beat up Sister Charles's nephew because he thought Momma was sleeping with him."

I jumped back like I was struck by lightning. "When did this happen?"

"A couple of hours ago."

"Is it true? Did she sleep with him?"

"No. I don't know. I honestly don't care anymore," she said with her voice cracking.

Suddenly, she sprang to her feet, pushing me out of the way and heading for the door. "I need to clean myself up. Can you give me some privacy, please?" she asked, opening the door.

I reached over into the tub, grabbed the knife and got up from the floor. "Okay, I'll leave you alone." I walked a few paces to the door and then remembered what I came in there for. "Promise, can you give me a quick second? I need to use the bathroom bad."

"Alright," she nodded, stepping outside the door. Once she was gone, I doubled back over to the medicine cabinet. Grabbing it by the bottom, I shimmied it off of the thick metal screws that held it on the wall, exposing a small square hole in the drywall behind it.

"So that's where he hides his money," Promise said, sneaking in behind me.

"I thought I told you I had to use the bathroom?"

"I knew you didn't have to use the bathroom because you're acting funny. I wanted to see what you were doing."

Embarrassed, I shook my head, "Don't tell your brother, ok?" I said.

"If you can keep my secret I will keep yours," she replied.

I laid the medicine cabinet on the sink, reached into the hole and took out a small Ziploc bag of coke.

"What does it feel like after you take it?" Promise asked, eyeing the bag in my hand.

"The shit is bad for you. Leave it alone."

"It can't be all that bad. You take it and you're alright. Let me try just a little bit?"

"Girl, have you lost your mind? Your brother would kill us both if he found out I gave

you coke."

"Well let him kill me then!" she shouted smacking the wall.

"Calm the fuck down," I replied placing my hand over her mouth. She quickly pushed it aside.

"You asked me why I started cutting myself?"

"You told me, it makes you forget about days like this, it makes you feel numb."

"That's not all…you don't know how it feels to be afraid do you? Well I do… Sometimes it takes me hours to fall asleep at night. I sit up watching the shadows sway from the curtains around my window, scared that one of them just might pop out and snatch me. If I'm lucky I dose off as soon as my head hit the pillow, but that's when the nightmares begin. That's when I see him, I can feel him grabbing and groping me ... His rough hands."

She began to sob again. Her reaction from this revelation was more profound. I quickly grabbed her some tissue to wipe her face.

"Who are talking about Promise? Is it your boyfriend? Did he do something to you?"

"No, it wasn't Brian," she scoffed, laughing through her tears.

"Well, who?"

She leaned close to me and uttered his name in a whisper. Awe-struck I gasped after hearing who the culprit was.

How could he? I thought as she shared the details of what vile things had happened to her. "You have to tell your mom about this Promise."

"No, it'll just make things worse. I'm dealing with it."

"Cutting your leg isn't dealing with it."

"Well maybe I can try something new just this once," she said motioning to the bag of coke in my hand.

Thirsting for it myself I couldn't think straight. I looked into her fragile eyes and began to feel sorry for her. After a few moments of seesawing with my decision I finally submitted.

"Ok, just this once. Go over and shut the door," I said.

She walked over and closed the door, locking it behind her. I picked up an old magazine from the magazine rack atop the toilet and began to tap the coke on it.

"Give me something flat to separate this," I said.

She reached into the medicine cabinet and pulled out a metal nail file. "Will this work?" she asked, suddenly turning around, knocking the coke out of my hand and all over the floor.

"Ah, shit! Fuck!"

"I'm sorry. I'll clean it up. Just get another one."

"I can't get another one. If I do, your brother would notice and he'd kick my ass."

"You don't have any more?"

"No, I don't, but I know someone who does. I can get it tonight but it's gonna take me a while to get back and your brother will be here by then."

"I'll go with you then."

"Aight. But if you start acting crazy we coming back. Deal?"

"Deal."

"Okay, let me make a quick phone call and leave a note for your brother. I'll meet you downstairs."

"Who you calling?"

"My, *um*, friend... to make sure she's there. Go on downstairs. I'll meet you at the door."

"Okay."

After she had gone, I went in the room and called my cousin to let him know what was going down. When I was done I left a note for Fred and we headed on our way. We made it to Tasha's house around 9:00 p.m. Judging by her lack of composure, she'd been drinking.

"Gurl, I'm glad you came back. I thought you might be on lockdown for telling him about—"

I quickly placed my hand over her mouth. "I ain't tell him yet. By the way, Tasha, this is Fred's sister, Promise. Promise, this my girl, Tasha."

Promise timidly stood by the door. Tasha looked her up and down like fresh meat on a hook.

"Damn. If this his sister he must be fine. Your mama got some good genes, gurl."

"Thanks, I guess," Promise replied, looking towards me.

"Tasha, you have any more of the stuff you gave me earlier?"

"Yeah, I got a little left. Why?"

"Let me have it. She wanna take her first trip to the moon."

"*Ha, ha, ha*, so she wanna be an astronaut, *huh?*" Tasha walked over to Promise, who was still standing by the door. She placed her hand on the wall above Promise's shoulder and leaned in close. "You know you gotta know how to fly the ship if you gonna be an astronaut," Tasha said with a seductive stare. Promise nervously turned away.

"Tasha, leave her alone and get the stuff," I said.

"Aight damn, I was just playing around. You know that shit makes me horny."

As Tasha walked into the kitchen, Promise asked, "Is she gay?"

"It's complicated."

Tasha came back in the room with a glass pipe. "*Uh-uh*, Tasha. Cut it up. She can't hit it that way."

"You said she wanna go to the moon. I just wanna get her there faster. Come on over here and sit next to me. I won't bite you."

Promise slowly crept her way to the sofa and sat down next to us. "Promise, this ain't like the movies. When you inhale, take it slow. It's gone taste strange at first and then you gone feel it." Tasha put the rock in the pipe and fired it up. She took two puffs and handed it to Promise. "Go head, take a hit," Tasha said.

Promise grabbed the pipe and put it to her lips while Tasha fired it up underneath with the lighter. Promise took a couple of short drags and stopped.

46

"This feels—fuck! I feel good," Promise said, leaning back on the sofa.

"We have blast off!" Tasha joked. Tasha handed me the pipe next. I took a few big hits off of it and before I knew it I'd blacked out... I woke up around 6:00 a.m. I was completely naked laying on the bed with Promise on one side of me and Tasha on the other. In a panic I shook Promise to wake her up. But she didn't respond. She lethargically moved away from me and rested her head on Tasha's chest.

"Shit, what have I done?" I said rigorously trying to shake her awake.

Chapter 6 - NICKY
Lovers' Quarrel

Andre and I felt sorry watching Albert walk out of the double doors of the city lockup. Although he only spent a weekend in jail, his weary demeanor made it seem like he was there for much longer. His wrinkled half-buttoned shirt swayed from his body as he drudged his way to the car. He got in and settled in the back, engulfing the car with a thick odor of cigarettes and musk. I cleared my throat, attempting to ward the stench from creeping into my mouth.

"I'll crack the window. We can use some air," Andre said, peeping over at me in the passenger seat.

Looking at Albert's bloodshot eyes, I could tell he hadn't slept since he arrived there. He sat in a somber silence, resting his head on the window as we started on our way back to the house.

"I'm happy to see you're alright, Albert. Did you drop the soap while you were in there?" Andre said in a joking manner. Albert smirked a bit but continued to gaze out the window.

"I hate to bring this up Albert, but Diane hasn't been home since Friday. Don't worry, we've had the kids and Diane's okay. I spoke with her friend, Mannie. He says that she has taken some time away," I said, waiting on his response. "You hear me, Albert?" He didn't reply.

"Honey, check on him?" I said, nudging Andre.

"Baby brother, listen. This might be what's best for now. Maybe you need a fresh start."

Still immersed in a zombie-like trance, he slowly peeled his head from the window. "You're right. She made her decision.

I can't try to fix it by myself no more. I have other things to worry about, like finding a place to stay," Albert muttered.

"You don't have long before you have to be out. Do you have a place in mind, somewhere that you can move in the next couple of days?" I asked.

"Not yet. I'll figure it out though," he replied.

"Well, in the meantime, you can stay with us."

"Thanks Nicky, but I don't want to intrude on you guy's space."

"Don't be crazy. You'll never find a nice place in a few days."

"I know Nicky, but…"

"No buts. You're family and I won't take no for an answer."

Andre looked back at him with a half-parted smile. "Al, don't argue with her. She won't let it go until she wins," he said. I gave Andre a swift punch in the arm. "Ouch! Well, you know it's true."

Albert chuckled, "Okay, Nicky. I appreciate it." He smiled at me.

Once we arrived at his house, we were greeted by the kids who were all waiting on the front porch. Overjoyed, Kanna darted to the car, jerked open Albert's door and gave him a tackle hug.

"Welcome home, Daddy. You stink," she said.

"I know, my munchkin lady," he picked her up and carried her to the porch where Fredrick and Promise were sitting.

"I tried to come get you out, Dad," Fredrick said turning away. Albert went over to him and grasped his chin. He carefully turned Fredrick's head back around, exposing his scraped and swollen face.

"What happened to you?"

"He got beat up," Kanna blurted.

"I ain't get beat. A couple of dudes robbed me the other night in Dreighton Heights."

"Where's your car? Did they take it?"

"Naw, it's in the shop."

"As long as you're alright, that's all that matters," he replied, boyishly rubbing Fredrick's head.

"Have you heard from Mommy?" Kanna asked. He sat her down beside Promise and Fredrick and stooped down in front of them.

"Your mom is going to be gone for a while. I'm not sure how long. In the meantime, we're going to stay with your Uncle Andre and Aunt Nicky until we find a place of our own."

"What are you saying Dad? Did Ma leave you?" Fredrick asked.

"He's saying he chased her away. I can't stand either of you. I wish I won't y'all's daughter!" Promise yelled, jumping up and going into the house.

"Promise, get your ass back out here!" Andre screamed.

"It's alright. She's got a right to be mad," Albert said, rising to his feet.

Over the next few days we all packed and prepared for our new living arrangement. Before we knew it, moving day was upon us.

It was the morning of the move and there still was no word from Diane. Andre dropped me off at Albert's house while he and Albert went to get a moving truck. As I began to turn the knob to walk into the house, Fredrick's car whizzed up the driveway. The passenger door opened and a pair of long slender legs stepped out. It was his girlfriend, Patrice. He raced off, leaving her there.

"Where's he going?" I asked.

"To the corner store to get me some cigarettes," she replied, walking into the house. Seeing her made it dawn on me that we hadn't told Fredrick that she wasn't allowed to live in our home. I couldn't put my finger on it, but there was something about her that rubbed me the wrong way. I followed her into the house and put everyone to work. Promise and Patrice began gathering what they could in the rooms upstairs, while Nina, Kanna and I took care of the rooms downstairs. I was in the process of picking up one of the boxes from the kitchen floor when a shard of glass poking from its bottom cut me. I jolted, feeling the pain from its prick, causing me to drop the box and shatter the dishes in it all over the floor. Blood began to trickle from my hand.

"Kanna, where's the peroxide and band aids?"

"Upstairs in the bathroom."

"Y'all don't touch anything until I get back." I wrapped my hand in a paper towel and headed upstairs. When I reached the top, I could overhear Promise and Patrice whispering in Fredrick's room. Clutching my blood-soaked hand, I tiptoed across the hallway and closer to the door so I could hear what they were saying.

"I need it, Patrice. Can you get me just a little bit more? I swear I won't take it anymore after this."

"Hell naw! Are you crazy? We almost fucked because of that shit the other night."

51

"I know. I'm sorry. It was my first time. I ain't mean for it to go that far. It's just I never felt like that before. Let me do it one more time before we leave, then I promise I won't bug you about it again."

"I said no."

"I can't believe you're treating me this way, after I've told you my secret. You're the only one who knows what he did to me. You of all people should understand how much I need this."

Leaning in a bit closer I caused the floorboards to creak. At once, the room fell silent. I began hearing the sound of footsteps coming toward the door, so I tiptoed back a few paces and waited. When the door opened I walked right past them with Patrice cautiously eyeing my every step to the bathroom.

As I stood over the bathroom sink bandaging my hand, I pieced together their conversation. *That project slut must've given her drugs.* I remembered the rumors that Andre shared with me about her. My first thought was to barge in and demand the truth, but I knew there was no way either of them was going to tell me anything, so I decided to keep quiet until I had a chance to confront Fredrick about it.

Leaving the bathroom, I went back downstairs and cleaned up the broken glass from the floor. Five minutes later, Andre and Albert arrived with the moving truck.

"The truck's outside. We have to have it back by six so let's hustle!" Andre said, dragging a squeaky red dolly through the front door. A few seconds later, Fred showed up. He came in the house carrying two plastic grocery bags that had water sweating from there sides.

"I got some freeze pops for y'all," he shouted inciting a stampede toward him. He pulled cigarettes from his pocket and handed them to Patrice. Kanna, Promise and Andre all reached into the bag and grabbed one of the frost-covered pops. After they were done digging he walked over and offered me one.

"I need to talk to you outside, Fred," I said.

"We don't have time, Nicky. He has to help us load this truck," Albert cut in.

"This will only take a second." We went around the back of the house.

"What's up, Auntie?" Fred asked.

"Does Patrice take drugs?"

"What? Naw, she don't take drugs."

"Don't you lie to me, boy."

"I'm not lying. She used to, but she stopped a while ago. Why you asking me?"

"Because I think she may be giving drugs to your sister. I overheard her and Promise talking about it in your room."

He pulled a pack of ruffled up cigarettes from his pocket, quickly snatched one out and lit it. His anger grew with each puff he took.

"I wanted to tell you before I told your father. You need to talk to Patrice and Promise and find out the truth, Fredrick."

"I'll handle it. I appreciate if you don't tell Daddy about it today. He has enough on his plate right now. I'll figure out what happened and let him know later." He flung his cigarette to the ground and went back into the house.

For the remaining time that we were there, Fredrick immersed himself in work, avoiding Promise and Patrice as much as he could. I watched him feed his brewing grief like coals thrown on a fire each time he tossed a box onto the moving truck. He labored steadfastly alongside Albert and Andre, loading box after box until the task was finally done.

The time had come for us to travel across town to drop their things off. Albert volunteered to drive the moving truck. Andre drove my car with Kanna, Promise and Nina, while I rode with Fredrick and Patrice in his father's car.

"Auntie, you mind if I make a quick stop on our way to your house?" Fredrick said, turning off the route.

"No, I don't mind at all."

"Where are you stopping?" Patrice asked.

Gritting his teeth, he snubbed her and carried on.

"You ignoring me now? Fine," she said. She opened her purse, took out a cassette tape, and placed it into the tape deck. An abrupt white noise came over the speakers, followed by a thump from the shrieking loud song that started to play.

The song was only on for a moment when Fred ejected the tape and threw it out the window.

"What the fuck is wrong with you?" she shouted, repeatedly slapping him. I bounced up towards the front and wedged myself in between them, forcing her to stop. As she continued to fuss, he pulled the car over to the curb.

"Shut the hell up and listen!" he shouted, smacking the back of her seat. Startled by his actions, she jumped back.

"Patrice, I'm gone ask you this shit only once, and I want you to be real with me. Are you using again?" He turned to face her, giving her a look that could cut through stone.

"Naw, babe, I told you I gave it up. I can't believe you asking me something like that in front of your aunt." Her chest started to surge up and down. She looked away, trying to collect herself.

"Why you lying to me?" he asked.

"I ain't lying. I'm with you most of the time. If that's the case, tell me when would I have a chance to take it, huh?"

"Maybe when you're with my sister!"

She gasped. Placing her hands over her mouth, she turned and looked back at me. I could see by her fright-filled eyes that she had figured it out. She knew now that I must have heard her talking to Promise. That look also gave her away to Fred.

"Get the fuck out my car," he yelled.

"I can explain. It ain't what you think. Your sister dealing with shit she ain't tell y'all."

"So you admit it? You did give it to her?"

"Yeah, but—"

Fredrick hit the back of her seat again, causing the whole car to shake.

"Calm down, Fredrick," I pleaded.

He hopped out of the car, went around and opened her door. "Get the fuck out," he said.

She looked up at him, folded her arms and sat there.

"Oh, you think I'm playing?" he yanked her out by the collar and pushed her down onto the paved sidewalk. She tumbled, twisting onto her side.

"That's where I found you, on the fucking street. That's where you belong, bitch."

"Fuck you, Fred. Fuck you and your family. I'm glad I got your ass jacked."

"What you say?"

"You heard me. I said I'm glad I got your broke ass jacked. You really thought my cousin was gone let you sell your

55

shit without consequences. How you think those dudes knew you hide your wallet in your boxer? It was because I told them where to find it. After Promise told me what happened, I knew your weak ass would go running after your daddy. All I had to do is make a call. So who's the bitch now?" she laughed, standing to her feet.

Infuriated, Fredrick ran to her.

"No Fredrick, don't!" I yelled from the car, watching him strike her. His hand connected with her face, forcing her back on the ground. I got out to push him away from her.

"I'm gone get my cousin to kill your ass," she yelled.

"I don't give a fuck who your cousin is. They ain't gone touch me."

She answered him, speaking in broken English and Creole. Then spit out, "My cousin is Yasif. You know who the Haitian is. You just put your name on the list. You dead, boy," she laughed.

"Fredrick, let's go, honey," I said, bringing him back to the car. We drove off, leaving her there. In a matter of minutes, Fredrick began to sweat. His hands were slightly trembling on the steering wheel. My concern grew even more.

"Who is Yasif, Freddy?"

"A guy from Dreighton Heights," he replied, shaking his head.

His eyes nervously roamed the streets, probing the cars that surrounded us during the drive back home.

When we made it to the house, Andre and Albert had already started unpacking the truck. "What took y'all so long? Where's Patrice?" Albert asked. Fredrick bolted into the house to find Promise. I rushed in after him. Once I got in the house I saw Promise backed into a corner by the steps. Fredrick grabbed her tightly by the arm and began yelling at her about what happened with Patrice. Kanna and Nina were at the top of the stairs, both screaming and scared. Alerted by the noise, Andre and Albert came inside to see what was happening.

"What the hell is going on, you two?" Albert said, prying Fredrick off of his sister.

"Ask your daughter. I'm in trouble, Daddy. I fucked up."

"What trouble, son? Tell me."

"It ain't nothing you can do about it." Fredrick yanked his arm away from Albert and left the house. Promise ran out the back door through our neighbor's yard. Albert and I went after her but it was too late. She'd gotten so far we'd lost her.

Chapter 7 - DIANE
Bellevue

What have I gotten myself into? I thought, pacing the floor of the shadowy room that had been my prison for the last two days. The only thing I had to keep me company was a trail of ants coming from a hole along the bottom of the pasty cement wall.

"Let me out of here," I shouted. I walked over to the graffiti riddled door and slid open the window to its food port. "Y'all let me out!" I repeated. Peeping out the crevasse I saw the nurse and an orderly coming to my door, so I went back and sat in the chair in the corner of the room. I had to act nice and calm for them.

"It's time to take your medicine, Mrs. Thomas," the nurse said, entering the room.

"I'm not taking that shit no more. It's messing with my head."

"It's doctor's orders, Mrs. Thomas. You can take it the easy way or the hard way. Do I need to ask Mr. Perkins to assist me?" she said, pointing to the orderly. Tearing up, I shook my head. "Well good then. Open up and take these pills." She gave me two giant horse pills. She watched as I put them in my mouth and washed them down with the cloudy cup of water she provided. "Open up and show me," she said. I opened my mouth and lifted my tongue while she checked to see that the pills were gone. "Good, you can close."

"Why can't y'all just let me go home? I'm good now."

"That's for Dr. Grimer to decide, Mrs. Thomas. You can discuss that with her during your evaluation today. You're scheduled to have it now. Mr. Perkins and I are here to escort."

"I hate that bitch," I sassed before I could stop myself.

"I'm sure she knows. Get your notepad so we can go."

I went over to the bed, retrieved my notepad and left with the two of them flanked on both sides of me. Walking down the narrow corridor toward the doctor's office made me nervous. I didn't know what to expect from her after the outburst I had in her office the day before. I had grown tired of the personal questions she asked and refused to tell her things that I felt were none of her damn business. She was the one who held the key to me getting out, and I knew if I wanted to go home anytime soon, I was going to have to learn to bite my tongue.

When we entered Dr. Grimer's office, she greeted me with the same zealous spunk that tickled my temper during my last visit.

"Welcome back, Mrs. Thomas. Hopefully you had a good morning," she said, smiling with her thin wired glasses hanging from the tip of a sharp nose. Following the same routine from the days prior, I shook her hand and sat in the chair next to her desk. She turned towards the nurse and orderly and said, "You can leave us. I'll be alright, Mr. Perkins," waving the nurse and orderly out the door. She then turned back to me. "Would you like some coffee before we start?"

"No, just get this over with, Dr. Grimer."

"Alright, suit yourself." She got a manila folder from her desk and sat on a small leather chair on the opposite side of the room. "I see you brought your notepad. Did you write in it at all?"

"How could I? I need a pencil. I can't use those crayons y'all gave me. I'm not a third grader."

"Pencils and other sharp objects are are not permitted to patients under your circumstances. I've had many of my patients write with crayons without any problem. I assure you that you can, too."

59

"That's because most of your patients are fucking lunatics, and I assure you I'm not," I said, mocking her.

She closed the folder and placed it on her lap. "Okay. Well, since you haven't written anything, I guess I'll see you tomorrow."

"What do you mean? I told you I couldn't write with a crayon. Why the fuck do y'all insist on keeping me in this hellhole?"

With a deadpan expression, she listened to my rant, scribbling words on the top of the folder. When I finished she went to her desk and picked up her phone. "Mr. Perkins, I'm done with Mrs. Thomas's evaluation. Please escort her back to her room," she said.

In the blink of an eye the door opened and in came Mr. Perkins to take me back to my room. As he got closer, I approached the doctor.

"I'm sorry for cursing at you, Dr. Grimer. I meant no disrespect. I just want to go home to see my husband and kids. You know I didn't mean what I said to the doctor last week. Having the abortion was emotional for me. I wasn't myself. Woman to woman, you understand, right?"

She clicked the button on her pin and scribbled a few more words.

"So does this mean I can go home?"

"Mrs. Thomas, understand that your doctor heard you say you wanted to die. He also caught you trying to steal pain killers that could've been lethal. Legally, the hospital has the right to hold any patient who threatens to commit serious bodily harm to themselves. Your actions are far from what we consider mentally stable. When we determine that you've made the necessary progress, then we will discharge you. Until then, do the exercise I told you to do. Writing your life story can help us identify together where things went wrong."

"Kiss my ass."

"Mr. Perkins."

The orderly caught me in the midst of bucking at her. He grasped my arms with a stiff grip and hoisted me out of the room.

"Kiss my ass, Dr. Grimer. Who the fuck you think you is? You don't know me. I'll blow this bitch up!" I screamed, furiously flailing while being dragged down the corridor. Coming to my room entrance, I grabbed the frame of the door and held on tight. The orderly struggled, trying to loosen my grip, his fat sweaty fingers slipping each time he attempted to pry mine free.

"I need some help on room seven," he shouted up the hall. Two bigger men rushed in toward us. They pulled my hands free, tossed me into the room and locked the door.

"Fuck you fuckers. Fuck y'all!" I screamed with all my might. "Y'all want me to be crazy. I'll show you crazy." I pulled down my pants and pissed at the edge of the door. It seeped under the door into the hallway. In an instant my door buzzed and the three orderlies returned. They put me on the bed and held me down, shortly after a female nurse entered the room with a long needle in hand. She swabbed a spot on my shoulder and slowly stuck the needle in. I hocked and spit at her, narrowly missing her face. The shot immediately started to take hold of me. I felt myself drifting off to sleep before eventually passing out.

When I woke up, I was lying in the middle of a padded room. It smelled like old bleached clothes. The room had a small barred window that let in the moonlight. Up toward the ceiling near the door I could see a tiny red light flashing. It swiveled every few seconds. I came to my feet and went to it. Once there, I could see that it was a video camera.

"I'm hungry," I said, looking into the camera and clasping my stomach. The door clanked and down came the window port, letting in a burst of blinding fluorescent light. A tray of food was

61

slid onto its platform and the slot was closed. "Thank you," I said. I took the food over by the window and ate it.

As I was finishing up my meal I began to hear rambling voices bleeding through the walls from the rooms next to me. One voice sounded like that of a younger man. "She should be coming home soon?" he repeated over and over again in a quivering manner. In the other room I could hear an older woman. She spoke as if she was two different people carrying on a conversation with each other. Both of my newfound neighbors went on talking for hours.

It was around midnight when the man's blabber finally faded. After I finished my meal I settled into my new bed. I lay there staring into the void thinking about my family until I eventually drifted off to sleep.

That night, I dreamt I was standing on the sidewalk in front of my home, although it wasn't the same relic that I was used to seeing. The house felt fresh with rich white paint and a bold red door. A lush manicured lawn drenched in thick morning dew stretched off into a jungle of bushes that wrapped around the porch. In the driveway, a handful of cars were parked; all of which were colored jet black with tinted windows. Behind me, a red car approached. It pulled into the driveway behind the rest of the cars. When its doors opened, Andre, Nicky and Nina got out. They were all dressed in white linen.

"Hey y'all. What y'all doing here?" I said to them, but they couldn't hear me. They continued walking to the house, so I followed. When they rang the doorbell, Patrice answered. She was wearing a black dress with a black laced shawl that covered her head.

"Come on in, we just starting," she said. The house was full of family and friends I hadn't seen since I was a little girl. They all aimlessly wondered about in a subdued mood. "They're in here," Patrice said, leading Andre, Nicky and Nina to a maroon veiled archway that led into the living room. She opened the curtains, revealing five closed coffins at the head of the room.

"I must've died," I said, watching on in horror. Out of nowhere, I witnessed myself walk into the room from behind me. I felt like a shadow observing its body. I was dressed in all black, holding a newborn baby.

"She's here," Patrice said out loud. Everyone responded by clapping. I watched myself walk to the coffins and stand next to them. Soon after that the crowd came into the room. A hole parted between them and out came Albert's father, pushing another coffin. He turned it aside, placing it in front of the others. Once he finished I handed him the baby.

"It's time," he said chewing on his pipe.

The crowd converged on me again. The floor beneath me started to tremble. Suddenly I had my hands wrapped around a gun with its barrel in my mouth.

"It's time, it's time," the crowd chanted.

"Don't do it!" I hollered at myself, witnessing the flash of the gun going off.

I woke up in a cold sweat. In panic, I checked the back of my head for an exit wound, only to find the bristles from my undisturbed hair. To my relief, it was morning. The sunlight that shone through the small window bounced off the white padded walls of the room, making it looked as if I was sitting on a cloud.

"Thank Goodness," I said, relieved that I had awakened from the nightmare. "Thank you," I said clasping my hands toward the window. A moment later the door port clanked and in slid my breakfast. I scuttled over to pick it up and found that my notepad and crayons were tucked beneath the tray. Looking down at them, I shook my head and thought about the dream.

"Alright, you win, Dr. Grimer," I said, looking up at the camera. I spent the rest of the day writing in the notepad. I started with things as far back as I could remember. Words began to spill out of me like an overfilled cup. I wrote and wrote until a new day had dawned. When I was done I had filled all 100 pages of the notepad, reducing the crayons to nubs.

"Tell Dr. Grimer I'm finished," I said, holding the notepad up to the camera. I went over to the door, slid open the slot and placed it in. Soon thereafter it was gone. The remainder of the second morning I sat under the window contemplating the dream. The images of the coffins were still fresh in my head. It frightened me so much that I didn't move an inch. Strangely, I felt a yearning to hear my children arguing again, I just wanted to hear them alive and well.

It was around noon when the door opened and in came Mr. Perkins and the nurse. Mr. Perkins was carrying two burly brown straps that were rolled around his hands.

"It's time for your appointment, Mrs. Thomas. Now, you're not going to give me a hard time today are you?" the nurse asked. I walked over, picked up the pills from her hands and swallowed them. I opened my mouth to show that they were gone.

"Thank you, Mrs. Thomas. Let's go see Dr. Grimer," she said, nudging Mr. Perkins. He unraveled the straps and followed closely behind. When we arrived at Dr. Grimer's office she'd just finished up with another patient. The young lady barged out the door, nearly pushing me to the ground. Dr. Grimer followed, stopping at the door. "Mr. Perkins, Ms. Green, see to it that Tiffany makes it back to her room. She may also need a sedative. Mrs. Thomas and I should be a while." The two of them left in pursuit of the young woman.

"Have a seat, Mrs. Thomas. We have a lot to discuss today." We went back to her desk and sat. She retrieved my notepad and handed it to me. "I looked through what you wrote, Mrs. Thomas. Thank you for sharing such personal things with me."

"You're welcome."

"I applaud your courage in telling me what you have, but in my opinion, there's something more you're not telling me."

"There's nothing more, Dr. Grimer. That's everything about me on those pages."

"Perhaps you think it is." She scooted from behind her desk and moved her chair beside me. "Out of everyone that you mentioned there's one person that stands out to me. Tell me about your husband's father."

The pit of my stomach dropped. Judging by the way that she was acting, I feared that she knew. *I was discreet about him; she couldn't have figured it out*, I thought. "It's not much to say. He's Albert's father. He took me in when I was a teenager. That's it," I said.

She reached out and gently held my hand. "Diane, you can speak freely here. All of what you say will stay between us," she said. I felt like a dam taking on too much water. I couldn't hold it in any longer. I swallowed back, working up my courage to say what she was waiting for me to say.

"Albert's father and I… we've been… we were having an affair."

She grabbed the tissues from her desk and handed them to me. "How long has it been going on?"

"I was about 19 when he first came on to me. He had a sickness, more like an addiction. He told me he loved young girls. In the beginning, it just felt good that someone his age would want to be with me. My parents had abandoned me, but he was there giving me the attention that I longed for. I knew it was wrong, but I was young and I ain't know no better."

"Did you continue to see him? Are you still seeing him now?"

"After my kids where born we stopped. By chance it started back up again about a year ago when his car broke down.

At the time I was lonely. Albert worked so much we never really saw each other anymore. One morning his father called our house. He said he needed a ride downtown to run some errands so I agreed to pick him up after visiting my girlfriend. We ended up spending the whole day together. It felt like my heart opened up again. Feelings that I didn't know that were still there bubbled to the surface. That night we had sex in the car. We were having sex all the way up until a month ago when I found out I was pregnant."

"Was the baby his?"

"I don't know. Maybe. I couldn't take that chance of it being his."

"Is that why you tried to kill yourself?"

"I tried to kill myself because I'm a worthless piece of shit. What kinda mother takes their rent money to pay for an abortion?" I cried.

"Diane, I have no doubt that deep down you are a great person. Albert's father is a predator who preyed on you when your mind wasn't fully mature. Whether you're aware of this or not, he has controlled you ever since you were 19. For your family's sake you have to be strong. Let him go. Tell your husband about him and keep him away from your family."

"No, I can't tell Albert. I won't. That'll fuck him up. He'll be in here like me."

"If you want to get through this, you're going to have to tell him. Not everyone gets a second chance to make things right, so stop running from your problems. Take hold of your life and confront them," she said.

By the end of the session, Dr. Grimer had earned my trust. It was the beginning of me opening up to her. Over the next couple of days I shared more with her. She used what I wrote in the notepad to show me the pitfalls that plagued my life, and more importantly—how to avoid them. By the week's end I had finally gotten to a point where she felt comfortable in releasing me.

It was my last day and I was missing my family something terrible. I hadn't seen them in over a week and I was ready to make things right. Fixing to leave, I quickly changed out of my hospital garments into the street clothes I arrived in.

"I'm ready," I said, Mr. Perkins opened the door and came in.

"Here are the rest of your things, Diane," he said, giving me my purse.

"Thank you. I hate to say it but I ain't gone miss nothing about this damn place," I laughed, looking about the white padded room.

"We ain't gone miss you neither," Mr. Perkins jokingly sassed. He walked me over to the main hospital lobby, escorting me right to the door. "Well, this is the end of the line," he said.

I reached up and gave him a tight hug. "Thank you for everything y'all did for me."

"You be good, you hear? Go on and get your family back," he said.

I opened the door and stepped out into the blazing sun. A brisk summer breeze blew through my hair as I carried on down the walkway. As I approached the end of the walkway I could see Nicky in the distance. She was standing in the emergency zone roundabout.

"Nicky!" I shouted racing to her. She looked back and in an instant hurried over to meet me at the edge of the emergency entrance. "Hey, I didn't know you guys knew that I was here. How'd you know I was getting out today?" I asked.

Her eyes welled with tears.

"You're not here for me, are you? Nicky, what's wrong?"

"Diane, it's Promise. She's hurt real bad."

Just as she spoke, the ambulance came in. Three doctors ran out of the emergency entrance to the ambulance doors. When they opened them, I saw Promise on a stretcher, covered in blood. Her face had turned pale.

"We gotta get her in trauma now. Her pulse is faint," one of the doctors said.

I ran over to her. "Promise, baby. Momma's here."

"Get back, ma'am. We're doing all that we can do for her right now."

"That's my baby! I can't leave my baby."

Nicky grabbed me from behind, stopping me from going any further. "Let them work on her. It's going to be alright," she said as I watched the convoy of doctors roll Promise away.

Chapter 8 - James
The Haitian

"One mission at a time," is what my coach said to me before boarding the flight home. It was our team mantra, our words to live by. Up until now, I had no idea how important that phrase would be to me. My mission was to get to my sister as fast as I could and pray that I wasn't too late. The three-hour flight home seemed endless. I was relieved when the foggy skyline of the city finally came into view. Once the plane touched down I jumped into gear, got my bag and maneuvered my way up the narrow aisle and out the door. In a full-out sprint I hurried up the jet bridge into the chaotic terminal where I frantically searched for Uncle Andre, who was supposed to be there to pick me up. Scanning through the droves of people walking every which way, I could hear him calling for me before I caught sight of him.

"J!" he shouted from across the busy room.

I spotted him and ran over to meet him. "Is she okay?" I asked, out of breath.

"So far nothing has changed from yesterday. She's holding on, but we gotta get back to the hospital," he said.

When we arrived at the hospital, we joined the rest of the family in the waiting area. They were tucked away in the back corner of the room, huddled together in a square they formed out of red benches. Each one of them appeared lifelessly drained.

"I'm so glad you're here, baby," Mom said, embracing me, followed by Dad. Aunt Nicky was stretched across one of the benches with Nina and Kanna fast asleep on both sides of her. I walked over and gave each of them a kiss, being careful not to wake them.

"Where's Grand Daddy and Fred at, Dad?"

"Your grandfather should be on his way. I paged your brother. We're still waiting for him to call the desk."

"Is Promise okay now?"

"She's in surgery again. They were having trouble stopping the bleeding. The doctors will give us an update when they're done."

"That's not like her. I just don't understand why she would do something like this."

"We don't either, son. We all are waiting for answers."

I sat down beside Mom and Dad, my eyes fixed on the clock. I watched the seconds turn into minutes and the minutes turn into hours, waiting to hear word from the doctors. Half a day had passed before one of the doctors finally came in to speak with us.

"Are you Promise Thomas' guardians?"

"We are," Dad replied, standing up with Mom clinging to his side.

"The good news is that the surgery went fine."

"Oh, thank God."

"But we do have a bit of bad news. The amount of blood she lost was significant, so much so that we found it necessary to induce her into a coma."

"What do you mean; a coma? I thought you said the surgery went fine?" Dad replied.

"Mr. Thomas, please understand that the amount of blood that your daughter lost could've very well affected her brain function. The coma was necessary to reduce the stress on her brain." Mom buried her face into Dad's chest and began sobbing.

"So when will we know if she's alright?" Dad asked.

"It depends on her vitals. It could be anywhere from a day to a week. We will have to keep her under observation to decide when it's best to wake her. Until then we're moving her to the ICU where you can see her within the hour."

"Alright, thank you, doctor," Dad's voice began to crack. He held Mom tight as tears started to fall down his cheeks like something I have never seen before from him.

Seeing Dad's reaction, the doctor turned and said, "For what it's worth, in many ways your daughter is lucky to be alive. In most suicide attempts of this type the patient usually severs the artery. Your daughter missed severing that artery by less than one centimeter."

"We understand. Thanks again," Dad said, wiping the tears from his face.

"That's not like her. Promise wouldn't try to kill herself. What happened while I was gone? Why would she do something like this?" I said as the doctor left.

"Son, the truth is your sister ran away two weeks ago after getting into a fight with your brother. Your Grand Daddy found her and bought her back to the house yesterday… She didn't say anything to us; I thought she was still mad. She went off and cut her wrist. We found her in the bathtub bloodied."

"What did she and Fred fight about?"

"I don't know. I haven't seen him since the fight. He's called the house a few times but hangs up before I can get a word out."

"Dad, that doesn't make sense."

"I know son, but none of that's gonna change what's happened. Let's focus on being here for your sister. We'll worry about the why later, okay?"

71

"Okay," I replied. Shortly after our conversation we received word that Promise had been moved to an ICU room. When we arrived at her door, we were paralyzed by what we saw. Tubes were intertwined all over her body. Her arms had swollen to the size of baseball bats. Her cheeks sank into her face. Gathering ourselves we all walked in together and assembled around her bed. Mom gently brushed back her hair and kissed her.

"What have I done?" she said. "I did this to my baby," she cried, melding into Dad's arms.

For the rest of the afternoon we stayed by Promise's side. Mom, who'd been overwhelmed with emotion, settled down on the bed next to her. She kept a steady grip of Promise's hand while Dad stood firm behind her. I sat across from them on the cold hard window stoop, helplessly watching the waves of my sister's heart monitor spike up and down. With every beep the contraption made it drilled the unwelcoming sound into my head like a stale song. After listening to it for a while, I decided to leave the room to get some air. A few moments later, Aunt Nicky came out and joined me.

"How you holding up?" she asked.

"I don't know, Aunt Nicky. I'm just mad with myself right now. If I wouldn't have left, none of this would've happened."

"You can't blame yourself, baby. You didn't do anything wrong."

"I just don't get it. I know Promise. She wouldn't try to kill herself for no reason. It's gotta have something to do with Fred. He must've said something to set her off. That's why he ain't here," I replied, pacing in front of an old vending machine. Two steps turn. Two steps turn. Aunt Nicky placed her hand on my shoulders calming me down.

"James, I believe you're right. What happened may have something to do with your brother," she said.

"How?"

"Walk with me." She led me down the hall. "A few weeks ago, I overheard a conversation between Promise and Patrice. They were talking about doing drugs. Promise also mentioned something about a secret she told Patrice, but she never said what it was."

"What? No. Promise doesn't do drugs. She wouldn't touch it."

"Maybe so, but that's what I heard."

"Where's Patrice? And how's Fred involved in all of this?"

"Patrice is gone. She and your brother got into a fight after I told him what happened. She threatened to get her cousin to come after him, some guy name Yasif."

"The Haitian? Yasif is Patrice's cousin?" I exclaimed.

"That's what she said."

The mention of that name made it clear that the situation was far worse than I thought. Yasif was the ruthless Haitian drug lord who controlled Dreighton Heights. When he first arrived, he gave most of the small dealers an ultimatum: work for him or get off his turf. Most of them joined his gang, but Fred didn't. He stopped selling in Dreighton Heights and moved to a new block a few miles away. He tried to keep a low profile, and for the most part it'd been working. Far as he knew, Yasif didn't know a thing, but if Patrice was the Haitian's cousin, there was something afoot, and whatever it was wasn't good. It was going to be hell to pay, and Fred had to know it the moment he found out about Yasif being connected to Patrice.

"This is really important, Aunt Nicky. Did Fred find anything else out about the drugs or Promise's secret?"

"No. He didn't say much at all to her that day. He just lost it and slapped the girl."

"This is bad, Aunt Nicky. This is really bad. I don't know if I can fix it this time."

"James, your father has been in shambles the last few weeks. He needs you right now. We need you right now. You've been blessed with a spirit beyond your years. If anyone can make this right it's you. You know where your brother hangs. Find him, bring home . He's the key to all this."

"No, he's not. Patrice is."

"How are you going to find her?"

"If she's Yasif's cousin, there's only one place she can be. Dreighton Heights."

"No, James. That girl already got your brother robbed and beaten at gunpoint; she could get you killed down there. You can't go."

"Auntie, I have to. Fred, Promise, none of us would be safe from this guy. I gotta find out what happened so I can squash it."

"No, James. If something happened to you—"

"I'll be alright. You said so yourself, if anyone can make this right it's me. Trust me," I said in a heartened tone, consciously looking her in the eyes. She peered right back at me as if she was waiting for me to crack and show my fear.

"Alright, I trust you," she reluctantly said before handing me my father's car keys. "I'll tell your parents that you went for a drive to clear your head. You be safe, you hear?" She embraced me tight and saw me off.

I reached Dreighton Heights at nightfall. Trying to avoid attention, I parked the car on the outskirts of the neighborhood under a splintered streetlight. It was a long walk to Yasif's hangout in the the middle of the projects.

The streets looked like something out of a war zone. Frames of old abandoned cars were scattered up and down the block as far as the eye could see. Overturned trash cans that littered the sides of the graffiti-tainted buildings were occupied by ragged cats fighting for food. As I inched my way through the neighborhood, an eerie silence besieged me. There was no one outside. In every apartment that I passed, the lights were off. It felt like a ghost town.

I was more than halfway there before finally seeing someone. It was an old man riding a rickety bike down the middle of the road. He had a long, braided beard decorated with bright, colorful beads. He wore a dingy brown shirt and pants stained with patches of black grease. I slowed my pace and carefully watched as he passed me by. As I drew closer to Yasif's, I could faintly hear music and people talking drifting now on the otherwise silent air.

The commotion was coming from the front of Yasif's building where a large crowd had gathered at what looked to be a party. I carefully crept my way into the crowd, unnoticed. The majority of the people there were teenagers. Some of them were dancing in the dirt-filled yard while others were busy getting high. Yasif had men posted around the building, keeping watch. There were two men patrolling the sides and four men who sat on the steps that led to the entrance. I shuffled my way through the crowd toward the stairs. When I reached the sidewalk, I felt a tug on my shoulder. I turned around to find it was the old man with the braided beard.

He let out a screaming whistle and then said in Creole, "It's an outsider!" while pointing at me. The music suddenly came to a stop. Everyone around me moved back while the four men came down from the steps and surrounded me. The meanest looking of the bunch stepped in front of me. He wore dark sunshades and had thick, long dreads.

"Who you be? Speak up now, boy," he said with a deep accent.

"My name is JJ. I need to speak to Yasif," I replied.

He took a drag off of his cigar and blew the smoke in my face. "Yasif not for you. You wanna taste, ah young boy? My friend take care of you."

"I told you, I need to speak to Yasif. It's about family. I ain't no crack head looking for a fix."

"Young boy gotta death wish, best be getting on before I make it come true," he chided. With a snap of his fingers he gestured to the other three to return to the steps. They walked off, leaving him and me in a standoff.

"I'm not going anywhere until I talk to him," I said.

"Okie," he said, whipping out a switchblade. I stepped back and looked for a place to run. "Don't worry, young boy. I cut you up real nice," he cackled, twirling the knife around his hand.

I ran for a small opening I saw between the buildings. I made it into the passageway and sprinted towards the back alley, but out of nowhere I was grabbed by a guy hiding in the shadows. "Where you going, motherfucker?" he said, holding me in a bear-hugging grip. I struggled to get free to no avail. The dreadlock man came over and pressed the tip of his blade along my chin.

"We fillet you now," he smiled. Right as he started to sink his blade, someone called out from the steps, "Pia! Yasif says bring him," he shouted.

Bloodthirsty, he grimaced and took the blade off of my face. "Don't get cozy, young boy. We scale you later, huh?" He flipped his knife away and pushed me up the steps and through the door.

Inside, we were surrounded by a smoke-filled haze that enveloped the foyer. The fog was so intense I could barely see where I was going. The stench of weed that filled the air was so strong I gagged, inhaling the vapors. The man in dreads led me through the cloud to the stairs where we went up three flights. At the top of the third floor we came to a door where two boys were sitting guard. Seeing us, one of the boys gave the door two swift knocks and then slowly opened it. "Go on," the man said, forcefully pushing me into the apartment.

The place was enormous. It looked like an old office that had been gutted. Strange pictures of exotic birds were hung on the walls. At the front of the room there was a large window that overlooked the parking lot. A life-sized wooden statue of a lion sat next to the window. In the middle of the floor, there was a lavish white sofa that took up most of the space in the room. The man in dreads walked me over to the sofa and instructed me to sit. He continued into a back room where I could hear people talking.

"The outsider is here Yasif," I heard the man with dreads say. Shortly after speaking, he returned to the room with a man in a wheelchair. The man's face was badly scarred. His left eye was covered with a black eye patch.

"You're the soccer player, eh?" the man in the wheelchair spoke.

"Yeah, how do you know?"

"How do I know? I know because I know everything."

"I'm sorry my man, but I came to speak with Yasif."

"I am Yasif," he quickly cut me off. "Not what you thought, huh, boy?"

"Naw. I mean, it don't matter," I stuttered.

He stared at me with a cold, dead glare. "Why are you here? Have you come to tell me where your coward brother is hiding?"

"No, I've come to apologize for what happened between my brother and your cousin. Sir, he meant no disrespect. He loves her. If it's possible, I'd like to speak to Patrice to clear things up." I swallowed anxiously while awaiting his response.

"Come," he said, rolling his chair to the window. I got up and followed. "Look out there. Everyone you see is mine. Here I am the President, I am king, I am the shepherd and they are all part of my flock. If I forgive your brother—show him mercy—how would that look to my people? That would tell them that anybody who wants to fuck with them can, and I won't do a damn thing! Is that what I should tell them, soccer player? Eh?"

"With all due respect Mr. Yasif, if you're the king you shouldn't have to tell them anything. What my brother had going is small compared to you. He's not a threat to you or your people and never will be. "

"Your brother was a fish on a wire. When I came here I gave him a chance to be a part of my flock but he said no. The coward wanted to be my competition. Every good businessman knows you gotta keep an eye on your competition, no matter how small it may be." He pulled Fred's wallet from his pocket, plucked a white business card from it and dropped the wallet at my feet. He took out a lighter and set the card ablaze. "I own this state now. Your brother's venture is over, now he owes for what he did to my cousin, and that debt can only be satisfied with blood," he said blowing the smoldering flame out and tossing it aside.

"If it's blood that you want, why not kick his ass and call it done. Hell, kick my ass; I'll gladly pay the debt. But you don't have to take his life. He didn't take a life. Your people would understand that. And you won't have to worry about him selling anymore. I promise I'll keep him away. You have my word. "

He wheeled his chair next to the lion statue and placed his hand on its head. Methodically he began to tap his finger tips on it, causing the thumps to echo through its hallowed shell.

"Your word means shit to me, boy. This ain't the soccer field. Around here we play for keeps. Pia," he whistled. The dread-man responded by pulling a revolver from his backside and aiming it at my chest.

"Killing me won't prove a thing to your people. In the grand scheme of things, all it will mean is that you can kill a kid in cold blood. I didn't come here to die. Whatever it was you wanted from my brother you must've gotten, so please leave him alone, and let me leave," I pleaded.

"As you said, soccer player. You'd gladly pay the debt, it's time to pay up," he replied.

"You're the coward, not my brother." I closed my eyes, preparing myself for the shot. The trigger cocked.

"Stop, Yasif! Don't do this!" a woman belted out. I opened my eyes to see it was Patrice. She walked over and kneeled in front of his chair.

"I did what you asked me to do. You got what you wanted. Please Yasif, let JJ go," she said.

He began to argue with her in their native tongue. Gradually she managed to sway him to a silence. Still fuming, he furiously peered up at me as I stood there awaiting my fate.

"Not many people come into the lion's den and leave, boy. Go now, and tell your brother he is retired. If I see him selling in my city again he's a dead man and so are you. Now get the fuck out," he said, waving me to the door. Patrice escorted me into the stairwell. The muffled noise from the music and crowd outside echoed from its walls. I walked over and leaned against the railing, trying to calm my nerves.

"I'm so sorry, JJ. I never meant for any of this shit to happen," she said shamefaced.

"Well why did it happen? Why where you with my brother if he was your cousin's competition?" I asked.

79

"It's complicated J," she came closer to me and spoke beneath her breathe, "A few of my cousin's soldiers were complaining about losing customers. It didn't take them long to find out that their business was going to your brother. Yasif wanted to cut off the head of the snake. If the product was good enough to take customers, he knew whoever controlled it was a threat, and he wanted to take care of that threat. You see, it never was about Fred, JJ. It was about his distributor. I was supposed to find out who it was. I thought I could get Fred to tell me, but you know how paranoid he is. He kept the information on the card in his wallet. The card my cousin burned."

"So you had him robbed and beaten for it?"

"No, they were only suppose to take his wallet. I didn't know they were gonna do the rest, you gotta believe me. I fell in love with your brother. I still am."

Deeply, I exhaled and said, "What's done is done. I didn't only come here for my brother. I came to speak to *you*. Patrice, Promise is in the hospital."

"What happened? Is she alright?"

"She's in a coma. They said she tried to commit suicide."

"Oh no," she sighed. "Is there anything I can do?"

"I'm trying to find out what happened to her that would make her do it, and I was hoping that you could tell me."

"Why would I know? You know your sister never talked to me much."

"My aunt told me about the conversation she overheard between you and Promise. She said you mentioned something about drugs and a secret. Please don't lie to me, Patrice. I just want to know what's going on with my sister."

"It's true, I gave her drugs to cope with her pain, but I'm not the monster that caused her to do this. The bastard you need to be questioning is your grandfather. JJ, he raped Promise. That was the secret she told me."

"What?"

"She was too embarrassed to tell y'all. That's why she keep it to herself for all this time."

How could I be so stupid? Since I was a little boy I had my suspicions, but I refused to believe it. The proof was always there in the open, evident in the unusual ways that he used to look at her. I ignored it all, hoping that the feeling would go away. I couldn't have been more wrong.

Armed with my new information, I hurried back to the hospital. When I got back to the room, I found Mom, Dad and Uncle Andre in the same spot they were in when I left, but Aunt Nicky and the kids were gone. I walked over to my father and handed him the car keys.

"Where are Aunt Nicky and the girls?" I asked.

"They went home to get some rest. Are you okay, son? It doesn't look like the drive helped. Maybe you should go home and get some rest as well," he said, firmly placing his hands on my shoulders.

"No Dad, I'm not okay. It's Grand Daddy. He's the reason Promise did it. He raped her," I said flat-out. Dad's arms fell limp.

"No, he couldn't have. He swore to me that he'd never do that," Mom blurted.

"He swore to you? Wha—What's going on, Diane?" Dad asked stepping away in confusion and a mix of terrible emotions.

Uncle Andre perked up in his seat while I stepped closer to hear what she had to say. Before she had a chance to speak, Aunt Nicky walked in the door.

"I thought you were staying at the house with the kids. Where are they?" Uncle Andre asked.

"Don't worry, they're in good hands. I was going to stay with them but your father stopped by. He's with them at the house. He insisted on keeping them for us," she smiled, not knowing the danger she'd put them in.

Chapter 9 - Andre Sr.
Hunter's Game

I love grocery shopping on the first of the month; it was the only day that the store was packed full of the floozies that I craved and today was no different. Like a beast stalking its prey, I pushed my cart from aisle to aisle, looking for some young fresh meat to pounce on. On the prowl, I spotted a tall, slender woman in the produce section. She was a bit old for my taste, but the glimpse I got of her nipples poking through a white spaghetti-strap top was hard to ignore. I hurried over, positioning my cart behind her. I trailed along, watching her smooth creamy legs switch back and forth, tantalizing me with every step. Entranced, I followed her all the way to the checkout counter. As I approached the cash register, I could see a familiar figure walking up to the lane next to me. It was Promise.

She moved by me stealth-like, quickly slipping out of the exit. I fumbled around my cart and pursued her out the door. "Promise!" I shouted. She ignored me and continued toward a metallic red car hovering around the parking lot. The car engine revved and drove over to meet her. She quickly popped open the passenger door and hopped in. The car revved up once more and took off towards the exit; they'd be gone down the street if I didn't hurry. I stepped into the middle of the exit lane blocking their escape. In a panic, the driver turned the wheel sharply and slammed on the brakes, causing the car to skid to a stop in front of me.

"Get out the damn car!" I said, slamming my hand on the hood. The driver looked over at her in disbelief. He was a young boy who couldn't have been too much older than Promise. She crouched down in the seat and palmed her face. "Promise, I'm not gon' say it again. Get out the car, or I'm calling the police."

She leaned over, kissed the boy on his cheek, and got out of the car. "Thank you, Brian," she said, closing the door. He screeched off like a bat out of hell, leaving us in a trail of smoke.

She looked like she'd just come from a night of partying. Her hair was frizzled and her eyes sagged. She had on a pink V-neck shirt with a tattered denim skirt that came down to her knees.

"Where you been the last week, girl? We all been worried sick about you," I asked her.

She didn't reply. She stood there with her arms folded, frantically tapping her foot on the pavement. "You ain't got nothing to say for yourself? Alright then, get in the car," I said. She snapped her neck at me and left for the car. I drove her to my apartment.

When we arrived, I began to have that anxious feeling that I'd often got around her, a feeling that had tormented me since the night I popped her cherry. Promise was one of the first young fillies that I'd ever fucked, and although I knew it was wrong, I'd been aching for another chance at her ever since.

"Why didn't you just take me home? I don't wanna stay here," she said dragging in the door behind me.

"It's too late to drive you halfway across town. I'll take you home in the morning. I reckon you better get settled in the spare room. I'll get supper ready," I replied.

She went aloof, drifting off down the hallway into the spare room. It felt like a special occasion so I made my favorite meal: fried chicken with green beans and mashed potatoes with gravy. I set the table and prepared our plates.

"Promise, dinner's ready!"

After a few minutes of waiting, she came out and sat by the table. She looked like a child who'd walked out into the cold without a jacket. Her petite frame shivered every so often while she brushed her hands over her arms, steadily covering her cleavage.

"Go ahead and dig in, sweetheart. I know you must be hungry." She picked up a piece of chicken from her plate and devoured it as if she'd never had chicken before. "When was the last time you ate something?" I asked.

"Yesterday, at Brian's," she muffled, scarfing down a fistful of food.

"Slow down sweetheart. The food ain't going nowhere," I replied, fixated on her lips covered in sticky grease.

"What?" she exclaimed, shielding her mouth with her hands.

"Nothing. I just love looking at you. You're all grown up now. I always knew you'd be a beautiful young woman."

Hearing this sent her into an uneasy fit. She hurried and finished the last bit of food that she was chewing.

"I'm done," she said, abruptly twisting up out of her chair. She grabbed her plate and took it into the kitchen. I got up and went after her. At a snail's pace, I eased up behind her while she dropped the plate into the sink. She turned around and jolted as she saw me standing there, towering before her.

"I wanna go home," she replied, "Please take me home."

She stepped back, inching her way closer to the sink. I placed my hands around her waist and drew her closer to me.

"I'll take you home sweetheart, if you give Big Daddy a little sugar." I worked my hands down the back of her skirt, attempting to lift it up.

"Please stop," she cried, pushing me away.

"I know you like it like this. I can still remember how you made Big Daddy feel. Come on, let me touch that pussy." I clutched at her panties and began to pull them down. She grabbed my hand in an attempt to stop me.

"Don't be like that, sweetheart," I said, prying her hands back.

"Stop!" she shouted.

We began to tussle. She clawed and scratched at my hand while I struggled to regain control of her. "Get off me," she huffed, fighting back.

Her panties started to rip. With one broad swing, she elbowed me in the stomach. The force from the blow dropped me to my knees. Seeing a chance to escape, she hurdled me and started to run. I leaped out and grabbed hold of her foot before she was able to catch stride. She tugged at her caught leg, trying to wiggle it free of my grip. With all her might, she repeatedly yanked until her leg jarred loose. The motion knocked her off balance and catapulted her towards the counter where she fell and struck her head.

She was dazed. She lay there stretched out on the floor, face down, groaning. Holding my stomach, I got up from the floor and stood over her. I kneeled down and touched her on the ass. She reached back to swat my hand away, but didn't have the power to push it.

"You wanna make a movie?" I said, panting. I went into my bedroom and got my video camera. When I returned to get her, she was crawling for the door. I picked her up, took her into my room and tossed her on the bed face down.

"Please, don't do this to me again," she murmured.

"That's why I'm taping it, sweetheart. So we don't have to do this again. I'll have you anytime I want you," I whispered in her ear. I went over and set the camera to record, pulled her panties off and began to thrust in her right away, I couldn't hold back. She tightened her legs, preventing me from getting all the way in. I grabbed hold of the back of her hair and violently yanked her head towards me. "Open your fucking legs or I'll make you."

She released the tension out of her legs and I pushed in all the way. Oh, it felt so good. I reached down and palmed both of her breasts. The sensation I got from touching them made me twinge. With every pump I took she squealed in agony. "Shut up, you little bitch," I said each time she wailed. When I was almost done, I pulled out and climaxed on her back so the camera could catch it all. Feeling this, she squirmed around to get it off. After catching my breath, I got up and turned the camera off.

I picked her panties up from the floor, wiped my dick off with them and tossed them on the bed next to her. "Sweetheart, I trust we can keep this between me and you like the last time, right? Nobody'll believe a lying runaway no how."

She lay there curled in a knot, sobbing. I got the camera and headed for the door.

"I'll be in the living room if you need me. Goodnight, pumpkin," I said, cutting off the light. I took out a bottle of wine, sat out on the sofa and drank myself to sleep.

The next morning, I woke up with a terrible hangover. My head spun so bad I could barely stand on my feet. The house was quiet. The only noise that pierced the silence was the wiring hum from the refrigerator.

"Promise!" I nervously called out. She didn't reply. I went back to the room where I found her sitting on the bed with a knife in her hand. "What you doing with that?" I asked. She looked at me with a blank stare. "Come on, I'm gon' take you home," I said.

Gripping the knife, she stood up and slowly began to walk toward me. "Promise, you put that knife down." Her hands began to shake. I took a step back. "Promise?" She continued to walk toward me. "You wanna kill me, *hum*? Come on; let me see you kill me!" I lifted my shirt and smacked my chest.

She stopped, leaving only inches between us. She stood there shivering. The knife swayed back and forth in her hands before she finally dropped it on the floor in front of me.

"Good. Let's go," I said.

I grabbed her by the neck and began choking her. "Don't you ever in your life raise a knife to me again. If you do, I'mma kill you, you understand?" I released her and pushed her to the door. "Now get your shit. Let's go."

She gathered herself together and then we left. We arrived at Andre's house around midmorning. Nicky opened the door, greeting us with her warming smile.

"Where have you been? We been worried sick about you," she said, seizing Promise and giving her a big hug. Promise pushed her off and went into the house. "Well excuse me," Nicky replied, watching Promise take flight up their winding stairs.

"Hey, Mr. Thomas."

"Hey, lovely. Give me some sugar," I said, kissing her cheek.

"How did you find her?"

"She has been staying with some boy. I caught her in Big Sam's grocery store yesterday."

"Why you didn't call us?"

"It must've slipped my mind, I guess. It was late so I just went home for dinner and bed. Sorry."

"She's back, that's all that matters. Now, if only we could find where Fredrick has run off to. I swear those kids are gonna drive Albert insane."

"Where is everyone?"

"Albert's upstairs with the girls. Andre's in the kitchen cleaning chitterlings."

Suddenly, we heard a loud bang and glass shattering.

"What the hell was that?" Andre said, whisking out of the kitchen.

"I don't know, Jr. It sounded like it came from upstairs."

The three of us went up to investigate. Walking into the hallway, we came upon Albert standing outside of the bathroom door.

"It's Promise. I tried to talk to her. She locked herself inside," he said in a panic.

Andre put his ear to the door. "I don't hear anything," he replied, wide-eyed.

"Get back!" Albert hollered, ramming the door open with his shoulder.

Inside the bathroom, the floor was littered with broken glass that came from the vanity. A trail of blood led from the sink into the bathtub. Albert rushed in, and as came upon the side of the tub, he collapsed to his knees.

"Promise? No, baby, no," Albert cried, lifting Promise's convulsing body. "Call an ambulance!" he yelled. The tub was filled with blood gushing from her wrists. On her lap lay a shard of glass smeared with her fingerprints.

Hearing the racket, Nina and Kanna came to the door.

"What happened?" Nina asked, poking her head in.

Nicky quickly covered her eyes. "Come on girls, let's go." Nicky grabbed the girls, went into the next room and called for help.

"Dad give us those towels. We gotta stop the bleeding," Albert said. I got the hand towels from the sink and threw them over. Both of them grabbed each of Promise's wrists and bore down as hard as they could. I stood over them and watched as she began to change from brown to blue. "Hold on baby, help is coming," Albert said in a shaky voice.

By the time the paramedics showed up, she appeared to be gone. Albert and Andre stepped aside and they went to work wrapping her wounds. In a flash, they had her up on the gurney and out the door.

"Let's go, y'all. Dad, are you going to ride with me?" Albert asked.

"No, I'll drive and meet y'all there."

"Okay," he replied. They loaded into their cars and sped off ahead of the ambulance.

I had no intentions of going to the hospital. Instead, I hung back and sat on the edge of the tub, looking down at my reflection through the scattered specks of blood-stained glass on the floor. I couldn't help but smile—thinking about the night before. I was eager to get back to watch the newest video in my collection and I took comfort in knowing that there was for sure no way she was going to spill our secret.

Chapter 10 - Nina Thomas
Day of Reckoning

Everyone was quite waiting in Promise's hospital room. Kanna and I shared a rickety old armchair in the corner of the room, while the rest of the family was huddled around her bed. Uncle Albert stood behind Aunt Diane with his arms wrapped firmly around her shoulders, trying to soothe her. Daddy sat at Promise's feet with his head bowed in prayer. Mom stood beside him while keeping a steady eye on cousin JJ, who looked angry as he got up and left the room.

"I'll be back sweetheart," Mom said to Dad before running out after JJ. Fifteen minutes later, she returned, pale-faced.

"Is everything all right?" Dad asked.

"Yeah, everything is fine. JJ went out for a drive. Poor thing needed some fresh air," she said.

"I wanna go for a drive," I babbled softly. Mom came over and gently patted my head.

"I know you're tired, baby. Hang in there, okay?" she whispered.

Daddy turned to us and said, "Nicky, go ahead and take the kids home so they can get some rest. I'll stay here. We'll call you if anything changes."

"Okay, babe," Mom reluctantly replied.

Inside, I screamed with joy. I was so excited I had to bite my lip to hold back my smile. I loved my cousin, but I was tired of sitting around and watching her lifeless body beep and not move while waiting for the worse. I wanted to go home something terrible and was glad it was finally about to happen.

When we got home, Mom ordered us a pizza for dinner. Kanna and I turned on the TV and ate in the living room. Meanwhile, Mom was busy rummaging around the pantry. She gathered some of Dad's old work gloves, a trash bag and a straw cleaning brush, then went upstairs and began cleaning the bathroom. We could hear her as she collected the shattered pieces of glass, tossing the debris into the trash bag. After that, she began to scrub, boring so hard that the brush sounded like fresh sandpaper grinding into wood. In the middle of it all, the doorbell rang.

"Nina, can you see who that is?" Mom yelled.

I walked to the door and looked out the side window, but couldn't see. "Who is it?" I called out.

"It's Big Daddy!" he replied with his burly voice.

I opened up and there he was with a half parted grin on his face. He was sweaty and smelled like one of Daddy's grown up drinks.

"Hey sweetheart, give me some sugar," he said, leaning down giving me a peck on the lips that I quickly spat away.

He went straight into the living room where Kanna was waiting. As soon as he turned the corner, she bounced out of her chair and jumped into his arms. He picked her up and twirled her around the room.

"I missed you, Grand Daddy!" Kanna said.

Mom came down, totting the jingling trash bag behind her. "With all the racket that's stirring up, I knew it was you," she smiled.

"I called the hospital to check on Promise. Junior told me you were bringing the girls home to get some rest. I was on my way to the hospital when I realized I couldn't stomach seeing my sweet Promise all hurt up that ah way. I figured I could stay here and watch the girls for you tonight if you want. Put this old geezer to work for change," he laughed.

"Oh, would you? That'll be great, if it's not too much to ask."

"It's the least I could do, lovely. It'll be a pleasure to watch my two princesses," he replied.

She can't leave us here with him, I thought. Grandpa always acted weird whenever he was around us. It was strange being with him and I didn't like it.

In a hurry, Mom dumped the trash and grabbed her keys to leave.

"Mr. Thomas, after they finish dinner, they're to go to bed."

"Why can't we go back with you, Mom? I don't wanna stay here," I begged.

"No, Nina. The hospital is not a place for kids. You need to rest in your own bed tonight."

"Your mom is right, sweet pea. You gotta get rest if you're going to grow and be a big girl," Grand Daddy replied.

"You two be good for your Grandpa. I'll be back as soon as I can," Mom said and left out the door.

After Mom's car drove off Grand Daddy pulled his pipe from his pocket, filled it with tobacco and lit it up. He sat down in the living room with us while we finished our last few slices of pizza. When we were done, he got up to leave. "I have a surprise for you two waiting in my car. I'll be right back." He walked out the door, rubbing his hands together like my daddy did when Mom would say he was up to no good.

"What do you think it is?" Kanna asked, bristling with anticipation.

"I don't know," I said.

He came back in carrying a round suitcase. He placed it on the floor in front of us and opened it.

"Ta da!" he sang, unveiling its contents.

"A video maker!" Kanna said, looking at the video recorder in the case. "Is that the surprise?"

"No. The surprise is we're going to make our very own movie."

"I wanna be a princess in the movie, Grand Daddy. Can I be a princess?" Kanna said.

"That was just the role I planned for you. Kanna the Princess."

"What's Nina going to be?"

"Nina can be a princess too, and I'll pretend to be a king. How's that sound?"

"It sounds stupid. I don't wanna be in the movie," I replied giving off a full pout. *Maybe if I'm grumpy he'll leave me alone.*

"Nina sweetheart, you have to be. You have the lead role. Now wouldn't that be fun?"

"I don't want to."

"Alright, well I'm afraid without Nina we can't make the movie," he replied, looking to Kanna.

"*Awww.* Come on, Nina. We never have fun. Just do it this once, please," Kanna said, tugging at my arm.

I crossed my arms, holding on to my decision. Kanna nagged me until I cracked.

"Oh alright," I replied, giving in.

"Yeah!" Kanna cheered.

"Good, sweetheart. I'm going to use the bathroom. Y'all stay put, we'll get started when I come back." He placed the camera into the open case, put it on the coffee table and went upstairs to the bathroom.

Kanna picked up a glass ashtray that was on the coffee table beside the camera and placed it on her head like a crown. "I'm going to be the pink princess. I'm going to have the power to fly, and sing pretty, and be able to turn stuff into gold so we can be rich," she said, marching about the room humming.

"Put that ashtray back before you break it."

"If I break it, I'll have the power to fix it."

"Well, put it back and use your power on something else."

She marched back to the coffee table. She took the ashtray off of her head but lost her grip. The ashtray slipped from her hands and fell into the camera, knocking it out of its case and onto the floor.

"Kanna! Look what you did," I shouted.

"I didn't mean to. It was a mistake, honest."

As I went to pick it up, the camera started whirring. The videotape inside of it was spinning. I flipped the camera around, trying to find a way to cut it off. That's when I began to hear voices coming from it. It sounded like someone was hurting. Curious to see who it was, I looked through the view hole. Inside, I saw the back of a naked man and woman lying on a bed. The man humped on the women while she lay there, making noises as if she was hurting. After the man got his finished, he stopped and got up. That's when I saw that the man was Grand Daddy and the woman was Promise. Shocked, I nearly dropped the camera.

"What you looking at? Let me see," Kanna said.

Suddenly the toilet from upstairs flushed. I quickly fumbled around, trying to find the off switch. We could hear Grand Daddy's footsteps coming out of the bathroom, and then down the stairs.

"There it is," Kanna said, pointing to a silver button on the top of it. I pressed the button and jammed the camera back into the case on the coffee table.

"Are my princesses ready to make a movie?" Grand Daddy asked, coming into the room. He caught us scrambling to sit down. "What were y'all doing?" he asked.

"Nothing," I told him out of breath. With a suspicious glare, he turned to Kanna.

"What were y'all doing, Kanna?" he asked in a stern tone. She shrugged her shoulders, looking at the camera. "Did y'all touch my camera?"

"I lied. I'm sorry. We where just... playing around. Kanna was chasing me around the sofa. Wasn't you Kanna?" She quickly nodded yes. "I didn't wanna upset you because you told us to stay put," I replied.

"Don't you lie to me again. You understand me?"

"Yes sir."

He picked up his camera, went to the TV and cut it off. He placed the camera on the floor beside it and turned to us.

"I tell y'all what. We not gonna make the movie about the princesses just yet. This movie will be about the king."

"Whatever it is, we'll do it. Won't we, Nina?" Kanna blurted.

"Wait a minute, sweat pea. There're some rules. The first rule is that you have to do exactly what I tell you. It'll be like playing Simon Says."

"I'm good at Simon Says," Kanna replied.

"The second rule is that you can't tell anyone about our movie. It's going to be our little secret, okay?"

"Grand Daddy, it's late. Mom wanted us to go to bed. Do we have to play?" I nervously asked.

"Your mom is not here. I'll let you know when it's bedtime. " Fearful of his wrath, I swallowed back more protests, not knowing what to say to him. "Alright, Simon says go to your room and put on your pajamas."

Kanna pushed me out of the way and ran for the stairs. I gathered myself up and slowly followed behind her. She burst through the door to our room and went straight to her clothes bag.

"I'm going to the car again; I left camera stand. Simon says when I get back, you two should be ready, okay?" he shouted from downstairs.

"Okay."

The door creaked opened and he left.

"Kanna, I don't think we should play this game with Grand Daddy," I said, watching her dig through her clothes.

"Why not?"

"'Cause we shouldn't, that's why." I went over and squatted next to her. "Kanna, in the camera I saw Grand Daddy doing something bad to Promise. I think he's going to try to do the same thing with us."

97

The phone rang. "Stay here. I'm gon' get it," I told Kanna. I went into Mom and Dad's room and picked up. "Hello?"

"Hello, Nina!" Mom answered, sounding scared. "Where's your Granddad?" she asked. "He went out to his car."

"Is Kanna with you?"

"Yeah, she's in the bedroom."

"Listen to me. I want you and Kanna to stay away from your Granddad. If he gets near you or tries to touch you or your cousin in any way, you call 911. You hear?"

"Why? What's going on? Is this because of the video he made?"

"What video?"

"He's got a video camera here. I saw a tape of him. He was... doing it to... Promise," I replied.

"No!" she shrieked. "Listen to me carefully. Can you get the tape?"

"Yeah, I think so. He's still outside."

"Alright, baby. Get the tape, and you and your cousin hide someplace he won't find y'all. I'm called the police. They should be there soon. Go ahead and hang up and do it before he gets back. Hide until we get there. I love you."

I hung the phone up and raced down the hall to get Kanna. She was sitting in the middle of the floor on her stomach, playing with the loose strands in the carpet.

"We got to hide. Come on!" I grabbed her and put her into the closet.

"You scaring me, Nina. I don't like the dark. I'm going to tell Grand Daddy when he gets back."

"*Shhh*. That was Mom on the phone. She said that we had to hide from Grand Daddy. I'll be back. Just be quiet, don't make no noise, okay?" I ran down the stairs to the living room where I picked up the camera.

How do I open it? I thought feverishly, juggling it about. I began to hear some rumblings outside so I peeped out the curtains and saw it was Grand Daddy dragging the camera stand up our driveway. I closed the curtains and wrestled with the camera until it finally came open. I plucked the tape out and went to close it, but it was too late. He was at the doorstep turning the knob to come in. In a panic, I put the camera back and hid behind the curtains. Through a small sliver of an opening in the curtains I watched the front door creak open. In came Grand Daddy totting the camera stand. He placed the stand at the edge of the living room floor and aimed it at the sofa.

"Girls! I'm back!" he shouted. He moved the coffee table aside, clearing a space in the middle of the floor. He stood there for moment, rubbing the crotch of his pants, staring at the spot.

"Alright, girls, Simon says come..."

He stopped in the middle of talking. His eyes were drawn downwards to the camera. I could see him growing angrier as he walked over and picked it up. "Those little bitches," he said, looking at the empty open slot where the tape was. He tossed the camera on the sofa and darted up the stairs. Once he was gone I poked my head from behind the curtains. I listened as he thumped and clamored from room to room. Suddenly, Kanna screamed.

"Come out of there!" he yelled. "Where's Nina?"

"I don't know." There was a smack. Kanna yelped.

"Don't lie to me. Tell me where she is."

"I don't know! She went downstairs," she cried.

"Why were you hiding?"

99

"She told me to. She said Aunt Nicky called and told us to hide from you."

"Get your ass downstairs," he said. They both came down and stopped in the living room. He shoved Kanna onto the sofa. "Nina, I know you're down here, sweetheart. Come on out." He walked over to the coat closet. "I promise if you give me the tape I won't be mad at you," he said, gripping the knob of the door. "I'm going to give you till the count of three. If you don't come out, I'm coming in. One, two, three!" He yanked open the door and pushed back the coats in the closet.

"Come out of there!" he screamed, tossing stuff around, terrifying Kanna who was crying uncontrollably. I stuck my head out from behind the curtain, waving her in to join me.

"Oh, Nina," she mumbled, and then placed her hands over her mouth. Grand Daddy stopped. He looked out at her from the closet.

"What did you say?" She froze in place with her eyes fixed in my direction. He slammed the door to the closet and came over to the curtains. "I got your ass now," he said, tossing the curtains back.

I jumped out. "Run, Kanna!" I yelled. He grabbed for me and missed as I ducked underneath his arm. I went for the front door, but turned back for Kanna who had run into the kitchen. When I entered, I found her at the back door. With all of her strength she pulled at the knob trying to open it, but it was locked from the inside.

"The keys are over the sink," she said, pointing to them dangling from a holder. I dashed over to get them, but Grand Daddy stopped me in my tracks. I backed up to door where Kanna had shrunk behind me. He had us cornered.

"Leave us alone. Your tape's in the living room under the curtain," I said.

Panting, he slowly walked over towards us. "*Unh, unh*, too late for that. Now I gotta teach you a lesson," he said, grabbing us both. He dragged us back into the living room and threw us onto the carpet in the open space in front of the sofa.

"Take your clothes off and lay on the floor," he said. Kanna and I sat there, holding one another, crying. He took off his belt, folded it and popped it. "I said take your clothes off!" he yelled. We undressed down to our underwear. He stood watching us, feverishly rubbing the crotch of his pants.

We lay on the floor, side by side. He flipped us onto our stomachs and took our underwear off.

"Please don't beat us, Grand Daddy!" Kanna screamed.

"I'm going to jail tonight. Trust me, I'm not gon beat you, sweetheart. You two gon be my last. Don't worry it'll be over quick."

He kicked my legs open, knelt down between them and began to undo his pants. I buried my head in the carpet and took a deep breath. That's when I felt him jolt backwards.

"Get the fuck off her!" someone said.

I turned around and there was my cousin Fred wrestling him off of me. His arm was locked around Grand Daddy's neck, choking him. Grand Daddy thrust back into Fred, causing them both to fall. A small, shiny gun flew out of Fred's pocket and landed on the sofa a few feet away from them. Eyeing it, Grand Daddy dove for the gun, but Fred snagged ahold of his waist, fighting to keep it out of his grasp.

"Get the gun!" Fred yelled at us.

"I brought you into this world boy. I be dammed if you take me out," Grand Daddy said reaching back for Fred's face, gouging at one of his eyes. In pain, Fred released him. Seeing this, I rushed over to get the gun. I picked it up and Grand Daddy swatted it out of my hands sending it hurling across the floor. It scuttled across the carpet coming to rest at Kanna's feet. Shaking and scared, she picked it up and pointed at him.

"Shoot his legs, Kanna!" I said.

He threw me to the floor alongside Fred, who was squealing in pain holding his eye.

"What are you doing, sweet pea? Give me the gun," he said in a cautious tone, slowly approaching her.

"St... st... stay away," she stuttered. The heavy gun bobbed up and down in her small hands. As Grand Daddy got closer, he reached out to her.

"Here, hand it over to me. Don't be afraid," he said. There was a pounding knock on the door.

"Police, open up!" a man hollered from outside. Suddenly, Grand Daddy seized Kanna, twisting the gun in her hand. There was a loud pop. The gun dropped to the ground and Grand Daddy slumped over and fell on top of Kanna, pinning her against the sofa. The front door came crashing down. Two policemen stormed in and came into the living room with their guns drawn.

"Let me see your hands," they shouted at us.

Fredrick and I put our hands up in the air. The first of the two kept his gun fixed on us while the second closed in on Grand Daddy, who was laid on top of Kanna. Her muffled voice cried out for help from beneath him. The policeman took out his baton and rolled Grand Daddy over. Kanna sprang out and ran over into my arms. She was bloodied all over but none of it was hers. The blood came from Grand Daddy, who was on the sofa holding the private area of his pants. "You little bitch," he uttered shaking.

"Is he the one who hurt you?" the policeman asked, looking back at us.

"Yeah, he's our Grand Daddy," I replied.

The policeman flipped him on his side and slapped handcuffs on him while the other gathered our clothes from the floor and gave them to us to put on. He next went into the kitchen and got a wet hand towel to clean some of the blood off of Kanna.

"I need a doctor," Grand Daddy begged.

"You can bleed out for all I care, you son of a bitch," the police officer answered. They got on their walkie-talkies and called for help.

A few minutes later, their backup arrived. A police officer took Kanna and me out on the front porch. We saw a dozen police cars drive up, and then two ambulances. Most of the policemen went inside the house, with the paramedics following behind. Mom, Dad and the rest of the family arrived just as the paramedics were putting Fred in the back of one of the trucks. Aunt Diane, Uncle Albert and JJ went over and saw him off while my Mom and Dad hurried over to me.

"Did he hurt you?" Mom asked, embracing me.

"No. I'm okay," I replied tearful.

Aunt Diane, Uncle Albert and JJ came onto the porch. Uncle Albert picked Kanna up and rocked her, clinging to her tight.

A large group of policemen escorting Grand Daddy's gurney started to trail out the front door. One of the policemen came over to us and handed Mom, Dad and Uncle Albert a card.

"We're going to need you to bring your girls down to the station for a statement," he said. Uncle Albert ignored him. His attention stayed on Grand Daddy. As they walked him down the stairs Uncle Albert bawled his fist and ran for him. Aunt Diane took off behind him in fast pursuit.

"You motherfucker, it was you all along! " Uncle Albert screamed, tossing one of the officers aside to get to him. With a broad swing he punched Grand Daddy square in the mouth, sending him tumbling to the ground with the gurney falling on top of him. Uncle Albert charged him like a bull, he cranked his leg back to kick him but was stopped by the gang of policemen who jumped in and held him back.

Grand Daddy held his face in agony. He moaned as the paramedics tried lifting his battered body back onto the gurney. Seeing their struggle, one of the policemen rushed over to help. He'd gotten within an arm's length when Grand Daddy snatched his gun from the holster and shot him. Next, he took aim at Uncle Albert.

"I brought you into this world. I'll take you out," he said and shot again.

"Get down, Get down!" the police yelled peppering Grand Daddy in a hail of gunfire. He jolted to and fro before finally falling on his back. When the smoke cleared Grand Daddy lay motionless on the ground.

"Help!" Uncle Albert screamed holding Aunt Diane in his arms.

In the middle of the chaos, Dad and JJ rushed to their side. She was gurgling up blood, struggling to breathe. Her eyes started to roll backwards. Uncle Albert tilted her head up and cradled her in his lap.

"She jumped in front of me. Why would you do that?" Uncle Albert cried.

"I'm so..." she mouthed and passed out.

"Help her!" JJ yelled at the paramedics, who were crouching over in fear. They quickly gathered themselves and hurried over to help.

"We need to get her to the ambulance," they said, pressing their hands on her bleeding stomach. They all lifted her and carried her to the end of the driveway where the ambulance was parked. Once there, they opened the back and carefully laid her on the metal slatted floor. Uncle Albert leaped into the cab and sat on the bench beside her.

"Sir, you have to go now. We have to get her to the hospital."

"I'm not leaving her," he replied, grasping her hand.

"Let's get a move on," the driver shouted.

The paramedic shrugged his shoulders, slammed the door shut, and they sped off into the night.

About the author

Devin Darnell has had a love for writing all of his life. He lives in Midlothian, Virginia with his beautiful wife and daughter.

**View other books by Devin Darnell at
www.funkyfingersmedia.com**

www.ingramcontent.com/pod-product-compliance
Lightning Source LLC
Chambersburg PA
CBHW030638130626
46552CB00002B/906